LAURA ELLEN ANDERSON

RAINBOW GREY

BATTLE FOR THE SKIES

For Janet.

Thank you for your kindness and continuous support!

Cloud-cat cuddles to you!

xxx

First published in Great Britain in 2023 by Farshore

An imprint of HarperCollins*Publishers*

1 London Bridge Street, London SE1 9GF

farshore.co.uk

HarperCollins*Publishers*

Macken House, 39/40 Mayor Street Upper,

Dublin 1, D01 C9W8, Ireland

Text and illustrations copyright © 2023 Laura Ellen Anderson

The moral rights of the author have been asserted

A CIP catalogue record of this title is available from the British Library

ISBN 978 1 4052 9885 8

ISBN 978 0 0086 2092 9

Printed and bound in the UK using 100% renewable electricity at CPI Group (UK) Ltd

1

Typeset by Avon DataSet Ltd, Alcester, Warwickshire

LAURA ELLEN ANDERSON

RAINBOW GREY

BATTLE FOR THE SKIES

Farshore

RAY GREY

A Rainbow Weatherling with the power to control another's magic.

LOVES Pitter Patter Pancake Day at Sky Academy.

NIM

Cloud-cat!

Often explodes due to a rare glitch.

Loves to snuggle up on Ray's head.

SNOWDEN EVERFREEZE

Snow Weatherling.

Loves to solve frost formulas.

Tries to use cloudulations to solve big problems.

DROPLETT DEWBELLS

Rain Weatherling.

Lives with lots of other Rain Weatherlings at Trickle Towers Orphanage.

Loves to splosh Snowden's sandwich.

PERCY WONDERWHOOSH

Wind Weatherling.

Likes to eat lunch under tables.

Can sometimes be a tad over-excited!

TORNADIA TWIST

A Rogue Rainbow Weatherling.

Wants to turn Earth into a storm planet.

. . . will be BACK.

GUSTY GAVIN

Wind Weatherling.

The Sky Academy librarian.

Always there to help Ray.

KLAUS BOTTOMLY

Human.

Loves aliens.

Reads comics about aliens.

CLOUDIMULUS SUBURBS

SUNKEEPER CONSERVATOR

FLURRY MOUNTAINS

SUNFLOWER FIELD

BROLLY LAN

DRIPPING DOWN VILLAGE

CRACKLING CAVES

VALLEY OF WINDS

COUNCIL OF FORECASTERS

SCHOOL FOR SUNKEEPERS

THE MILL

SKY ACADEMY

SUN SUITES

FOREST OF FAHRENHEITS

WEATHERSTONE CIRCLE

TICKLE TOWERS

SUN CITADEL

CITY of CELESTIA

BOLT BUILDINGS

WINDVANE VILLAGE

THE JUMPING PUDDLES

AIRY APARTMENTS

WINDSOCK WEATHER WOBBLER ARENA

EVERY CLOUD

GALES & PRECIPICES

A COLD SPELL

RAINING CHAMPION

RISING BUN BAKERY

SILVER LINING

THE WEATHERLANDS

CHAPTER 1
FrEEziNG PoINT

Ray Grey twiddled her long blue streak of hair and stared out of the classroom window at the glistening Forest of Fahrenheits. She was finding it hard to listen to Mr Current, her teacher, who was droning on and on about the scientific formula for frost. Ray had bigger things on her mind. And it wasn't just the floofy cloud-cat curled up on her head.

Ray tickled Nim's cloudy bottom and his poofy tail swished softly across her face. He purred merrily and exploded, which was something he did a lot. Nim was Ray's cloud-cat and had been born with a rare glitch that made him explode frequently. But she loved him with all of her heart.

Ray's friend Droplett Dewbells groaned. 'I wish I was a cloud-creature. They don't have to learn about impossible frost formulas and useless

1

freezing points.' She wriggled in the chair next to Ray, making her rain cape sprinkle water all over the desk.

Ray LOVED school and learning about how all the different weather worked in the world: how the Council of Forecasters planned each and every drop of rain, flurry of snow or the zip-zap-grumble-rumble of thunder and lightning; or how the mighty SunKeepers used their magic to keep the big, glowing Sunflower in the sky glowing brightly. Even though weather magic was in Ray's blood, it still fascinated her.

But today Ray's mind kept drifting to Tornadia Twist – the worst Weather Rogue in history. Tornadia wanted to destroy the Weatherlands and become Storm Queen, and recently she'd almost succeeded. Ray and her friends had faced the ferocious fiend only weeks ago, fighting together using their weather magic. Ray had eventually trapped Tornadia in a puddle portal just long enough to break her Forbidden Spell.

Now nobody knew where the Rogue was,

or when she would strike again. But they knew one thing for sure . . . Tornadia Twist would be back. And she would have an even BIGGER and BADDER plan to destroy the Weatherlands.

'*Surely* we shouldn't have to learn boring frost stuff when Tornadia Twist is out there plotting to unleash a super storm?' Droplett said, scribbling angrily on her notebook. 'Next time I see that Rogue I'll make sure I splosh her right in the –'

'Shhhhhhhhh!' hissed Snowden Everfreeze, who was sitting on Ray's other side. His white mop of hair was frizzier than usual, and streams of snowflakes poured from his ears: a common occurrence when he was thinking. 'I can't concentrate with you talking.' Snowden adjusted his snow gloves, making the embroidery glimmer in the sunlight pouring through the classroom window.

'How can you think about schoolwork at a time like this, snow-it-all?! The worst Rogue in history could pounce any day now. The Rogue who took away the magic of a WHOLE clan of

3

Weatherlings . . . the Rogue who returned *after a thousand years* . . . the Rogue who almost killed Ray and is about to try to end the WORLD, and you're worried about missing Mr Current drone on about frost formulas?!' Droplett finally took a breath.

Snowden tilted his head a little and frowned at Droplett. '*Everybody* should know their frost formulas. It's the basis for most cloudulations. Once you know the freezing point of the frost formula, you can pretty much work out *any* weather equation, making complicated weather magic much easier. Such as the kind of complicated magic that MIGHT help defeat a baddie like Tornadia!'

Droplett looked at Snowden blankly then flicked her cape, showering him with rainwater. Snowden sighed and Ray stifled a giggle.

Snowden and Droplett were Ray's best friends in the entire sky. But as different as the two were, they shared qualities of loyalty and kindness. The three friends had been through a lot since Ray

4

had discovered she was a Rainbow Weatherling:
the only one in the whole world and able to make
weather magic that hadn't been seen for
a thousand years!

Ray had a golden winged staff that
produced colourful rainbows and
could be used to take control of
another Weatherling's magic.

Rainbow Weatherlings of the
past often used their magic to stop
dangerous Rogues who did everything
they could to break the rules. Weather Rogues
conjured their magic without an instrument,
making it much more dangerous and chaotic.
But a Rainbow Weatherling could take control
of a Rogue's destructive magic and transform
hurricanes into a pleasant breeze, vicious ice
storms into beautiful snow flurries and the
densest fog into a light, sparkly mist. It was an
extraordinary power!

Then along came Tornadia Twist. A thousand
years ago she unleashed a terrible substance

5

called Shadow Essence, absorbing ALL the rainbow weather magic in existence. And now she was back and determined to take away Ray's magic, but Ray didn't know why. All she knew was she had to find out what made her such a big threat, so she could use the knowledge to defeat Tornadia once and for all!

Droplett tapped on Snowden's page of neat equations. 'How above Earth do you think these *cloudiddli-oosions*, or whatever they're called, will help *defeat* Tornadia?' Snowden opened his mouth to speak, then furrowed his eyebrows. 'I still haven't worked that out.'

He sighed. 'I just want to help in some way.'

Ray smiled. 'You ALWAYS help, Snowden,' she replied. 'Without you and Droplett, I'd never have been able to trap Tornadia in that big, fat puddle!'

'Yup!' Droplett agreed. 'We are pretty awesome friends to have around.' She winked.

'But what will we do when Tornadia comes back?' said Snowden, looking concerned.

Ray grimaced as Nim burrowed into her belly and purred gently. 'Don't worry, Nim. I'm gonna make sure she doesn't win . . . THIS time, I'll make sure that stinker of a Rogue is gone for GOOD.' She clenched her fists. Nim farted in response, before exploding.

'Wow, Ray, that's fierce talk for you,' chuckled Snowden.

'I didn't mean GONE as in dead . . . just, y'know, locked away in Precipatory Prison forever – that kind of gone,' Ray replied with a grin.

'Now, class, an important note before you leave for lunch,' called out Mr Current – or as Droplett preferred to call him: the most boring teacher in the sky.

'Please, oh please, oh pleeease, say no homework,' Ray whispered.

But – despite all that was going on – Mr Current wasn't letting them off so lightly!

'Your task is to revise for your end of year temperature test in two weeks . . .'

This was followed by an audible groan from the class, apart from Snowden who was grinning from ear to ear.

'I LOVE revision!' he whispered.

As the friends entered the Lower Lunch Lagoon, Ray's nostrils were filled with the sweet scent of pancakes.

'I completely forgot it was Pitter Patter Pancake Day!' she said happily as they weaved their way around icy chairs and tables set out in rows, surrounded by sparkling sunflower lanterns and a warm breeze.

8

The friends went to join the queue and Ray began twiddling her strand of blue hair.

'Raaaaay, you're worrying about something,' said Droplett, pointing to the tangled threads between Ray's fingers.

'Well, of course she is, we're ALL worrying,' Snowden interjected. 'The Earth and skies are in danger of being taken over by a terrible villain.'

'I just WISH I could help get rid of Tornadia,' Ray whispered, feeling the frustration bubble up in her chest. 'We're not allowed to leave Sky Academy without a grown-up, we're stuck at ground level and I can't even sneak out because the school is completely *surrounded* by Weather Warriors.'

Ray nodded towards the window where her dad, Haze Grey, was perched upon his cloud-whale Waldo, a curly crook braced in one hand. He caught Ray's eye and waved frantically, almost falling off the cloud-creature. Ray returned a small wave. She loved her dad to bits, but wished he wasn't watching over her every second of the day.

9

Since the return of Tornadia, the Weather Warriors were *everywhere*. Every move, every step, every waft, wisp and walk were being carefully monitored.

'At least the Weatherlands are more prepared than last time,' said Snowden. 'I know your powers are super awesome, Ray, but you can't go putting yourself in danger by trying to face that Rogue on your own!'

Droplett nodded. 'We will ALWAYS be by your side to help.'

Ray smiled wide, then wrapped her arms around Snowden and Droplett. 'We're in this together . . . NO MATTER WHAT!'

Each of the friends reached for a plate of steaming pancakes before flooding the sweet stacks with an even sweeter bright blue skyberry syrup.

'What do they put in these pancakes to make them SO good?!' said Droplett through a mouthful, as the friends sat down at one of the ice tables.

'It's a mystery,' said Snowden. 'But perhaps it's best we don't know . . . I swear it makes them taste even better.'

'Mystery . . .' Ray gasped. 'Guys. You've given me an excellent IDEA . . .'

CHAPTER 2
THE PLAN

Ray leaned in closer to her friends. 'Remember, I have a *mystery* gift that Tornadia is scared of. I just don't know what it is yet . . .'

There was an excitable squeal from under the table, which made the friends jump. Ray peered below the icy surface to see a curly haired Wind Weatherling sitting with a plate of pancakes on his lap and syrup around his mouth.

'Um, Percy?' said Ray. 'Why are you under the table?'

'I like to eat lunch in a new location every day,' he said, rubbing the top of his head. 'It gives me a different perspective on life. Yesterday I sat in the Humidity Chamber, but I do not recommend that. My sandwiches were very sweaty. And so was my bottom.'

13

'Suddenly I don't fancy my pancakes . . .' said Snowden, pushing his plate away.

Percy Wonderwhoosh clambered his way up on to the ice benches, sitting as close to Ray as he could. Percy was a BIG fan of Ray, and always had a LOT of questions about her rainbow weather magic. 'So, what's your plan?! You have a MYSTERY GIFT?' he bellowed loudly.

'Dude, keep your voice down!' Droplett hissed, flicking a raindrop at Percy's nose.

Ray smiled patiently. 'If I tell you, you have to promise not to tell anyone,' she said, and Percy nodded so hard Ray worried his head might drop off.

'OK . . . so, every Rainbow Weatherling was born with an extra ability – a unique *gift* that they were named after, like Rainbow Slide, or Rainbow Bubble, or Rainbow Reveal. They could all do something different with their special rainbow gifts.'

'What's your unique gift then?' asked Percy. 'If you're called Rainbow GREY, then . . .' He

14

paused and frowned. 'You make stuff . . . *grey*?'

Ray burst out laughing. 'I decided to keep my family surname "Grey" because, well, I don't have just one gift. I'm a little different to the usual Rainbow Weatherling. When I received the power trapped inside the shadow crystal during the last Eclipse, the magic of EVERY ancient Rainbow Weatherling went inside me . . . which means I got ALL their unique gifts.'

'NO WAY,' shrieked Percy. Then he finally whispered, 'But why are you keeping it secret?'

'That's not the secret part,' Ray chuckled. 'When Tornadia trapped us in the mill after cloud-napping all the cloud-creatures, she said there was only ONE Rainbow Weatherling she had ever been bothered about, because he had the most POWERFUL of all the rainbow gifts.'

'Who?' asked Percy.

'My ancestor . . . Rainbow Beard. I don't know WHAT his unique gift is, but if it bothered Tornadia a thousand years ago I *need* to find out what it is now, and how to use it.'

15

Percy tilted his head to one side. 'Wait . . . did you say Rainbow *Beard*?' He erupted with giggles. 'How is a magical gift to do with beards gonna stop Tornadia?!'

'I was wondering the same thing,' said Ray. 'When I spoke to my great ancestor in the Aurora –'

'Wait, WHAT?' Percy interrupted, spitting out a whole mouthful of half-chewed pancake, much to Snowden's disgust. 'You spoke to your ancestor in the AURORA?! How?!'

'I don't really have time to explain all that,' said Ray awkwardly. 'Let's just say, I kind of, maybe . . . *died* a teensy bit . . . for a *little* while, when I broke Tornadia's Forbidden Spell.'

'Dabbling in forbidden magic is also why some of Ray's hair is black and white!' said Droplett, looking impressed. Ray took a deep, shaky breath, thinking of her friend La Blaze who had sacrificed herself to bring Ray back, and lost her own life doing so.

'My ancestor told me that the name Rainbow

Beard was just a cover up; that his true gift was a secret among the Rainbow Weatherlings.' Ray looked at her friends. 'It's the only thing that threatens Tornadia's evil plans.' She held each of their hands. 'So, together, we HAVE to find out what it is!'

17

CHAPTER 3
PANCAKE TRUCE

Percy placed a hand on Ray and Droplett's.
'It would be my HONOUR to help you,' he
said determinedly.

Ray thought fast. 'Um, Percy, you're a great
friend,' she said, 'but it's going to be very
dangerous and I can't risk you getting hurt!'

Percy looked a little glum. 'BUT,' Ray added,
'you can be our lookout here – make sure we
don't get caught, while we carry out our secret
plan.'

Percy grabbed Ray's hand again and shook it
vigorously. 'YOU CAN COUNT ON ME,' he said
very loudly, attracting the attention of a few of the
other students sitting on nearby tables.

Droplett splashed Percy with a few of her
raindrops. 'Remember, you have to make sure
you're not a blabbermouth, OK?'

Percy pulled an invisible zip across his lips and nodded.

'So, how are we going to find out what Rainbow Beard's gift actually IS?' said Snowden, unwrapping an extra drizzly drizzle-pickle sandwich.

Ray sighed. 'That's the problem. I have no idea, nor how to use it when we do.'

'You'll find it, Ray!' said Percy enthusiastically. 'You always work things out in the end.'

Ray loved Percy's positivity. 'You're right, Percy, I will!' she said with confidence.

But then the positivity was turned upside down and inside out when two of Ray's least favourite people came running into the lunch hall . . . Frazzle and Fump Striker.

Ray watched as they stumbled over to the counter looking like they were almost out of energy.

Frazzle Striker's strained voice was carried along in the balmy breeze that wafted around the

20

room. 'Where are the Pitter Patter Pancakes?!'

'Don't say we're too late, for thundering sakes!' finished Fump.

'All gone,' said the lunch lady. 'We only have gale-force gruel left on the menu.'

'That's strange,' Snowden pondered. 'On Pitter Patter Pancake Day, there's usually an endless supply.'

Another student marched up behind the twins. 'Excuse me, when can we expect more pancakes to arrive?'

'They won't,' said the lunch lady with a shrug. 'Slap and Streak from the Rising Bun Bakery never turned up with the second batch.'

'That's not like them,' mumbled Ray. 'Slap and Streak always bring enough pancakes for everyone on Pitter Patter Pancake Day.'

'Oh well, at least WE got some pancakes,' said Droplett, tucking into her tasty stack.

Ray watched as Frazzle and Fump walked away from the counter with their bowls of gale-force gruel. NOBODY liked gale-force gruel. It always

21

caused mega gale-force farts that often sent you flying forward at super speed. Not ideal.

The twins sat down at a small table in the corner of the Lunch Lagoon by themselves. As awful as they were, Ray couldn't help feeling sorry for them.

'I'll be right back,' she said, getting up and walking over to the twins. 'Hey, Frazzle. Hey, Fump,' she said, giving them a small wave. The twins' expressions looked just as shocked as Snowden and Droplett's.

Ray twiddled her blue streak of hair. 'I wondered if you wanted to sit with us and share my pancakes?' she said.

'WHAT?' cried Droplett, Snowden, Frazzle and Fump, all at the same time. Nim, who was hovering in the air on the look out for any stray crumbs, promptly exploded.

'NO!' said Frazzle coldly. 'We DON'T want to sit –'

But Fump elbowed his sister. Frazzle's tummy gurgled violently as the gale-force gruel got to work. Her expression softened.

'Fine,' said Frazzle. 'But just for a bit . . .' She got up and marched towards a VERY baffled Droplett, Snowden and preoccupied Percy, who watched as Nim reformed into the shape of a donut. Everything felt really quite strange. Frazzle and Fump sat at the edge of the icy bench and Ray slid her plate of pancakes over to them.

Fump didn't hesitate. He shoved a whole pancake in his mouth. Frazzle nibbled at the edges of another, then gradually the bites got bigger and bigger and it was gone in seconds.

'YUM!' said Fump through a mouthful. 'I wish I could eat pancakes ALL DAY!'

Frazzle raised an eyebrow. 'I guess you're not THAT bad, Ray Grey . . .' She even smiled a little!

Ray grinned widely like a goon but, just at that very moment, the Lunch Lagoon was plunged into pitch-blackness. There was a POOF as Nim exploded again.

'Either the light just disappeared . . . or I REALLY need to upgrade my glasses,' said Snowden.

'It never gets dark in the Weatherlands unless there's an Eclipse,' said Droplett's voice.

'I didn't think we were due an Eclipse for another eleven years?' Percy squeaked.

'You're both right,' Ray gulped. 'But I don't think this has anything to do with an Eclipse . . .'

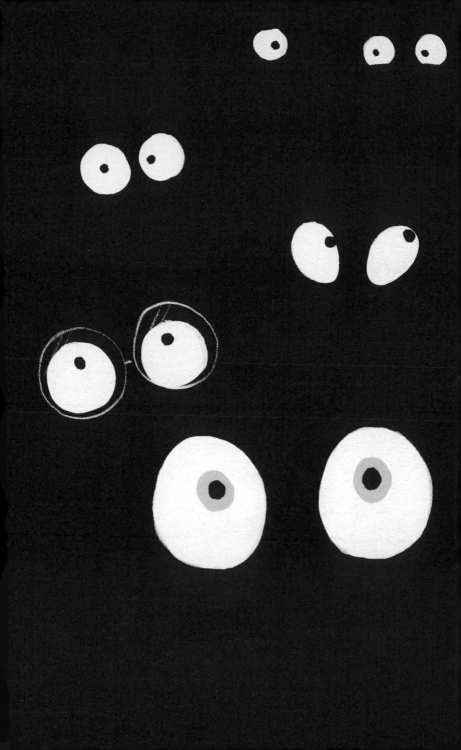

CHAPTER 4
IT BEGINS . . .

There was a swish followed by an almighty SPLOSH.

'Droplett!' cried Snowden. 'You've soaked my sandwich AGAIN.'

'Your sandwich is the least of our worries right now,' Droplett replied. 'The big Sunflower in the sky has STOPPED SHINING.'

Plates smashed and food squelched as the pupils panicked and scrambled about the dark room in a frenzy.

Ray thought fast, pulling out the winged staff from the back of her waistcoat. Luckily she had been practising her special rainbow gifts every single day, before and after school . . . as well as reading up on them in bed and getting up extra early in the mornings. Remembering Rainbow Light's gift, Ray tapped her staff on the ground twice, activating an illuminated rainbow halo at its top. 'Quick!' she said to the anxious children. 'Gather round me.'

Soon, everyone in the Lunch Lagoon was huddled around the rainbow-haired girl, including the lunch ladies.

'Children!' came the voice of the head teacher Miss Glacielle. She emerged from the darkness, her eyes wide with fear.

'If there's one thing I really hate,' said Snowden, 'it's seeing a teacher look scared. I didn't think teachers *ever* got scared.'

Miss Glacielle made her way into the centre of the crowd. 'Thank you, Ray,' she said before addressing everyone else. 'Please remain calm, children.'

'But Miss, what's happening?!' cried a rain student.

'Are we in danger?'

'I want my mum!'

'Please, everyone, listen to me. I want you all to form an orderly line and follow me up to the

28

Sky Dome,' said Miss Glacielle. 'Ray Grey, if you wouldn't mind guiding us with your rainbow light?'

Ray nodded and held up her staff a little higher so everyone could see the shiny halo at its top.

She led the way, walking carefully up the many staircases, through tree tunnels and across thick branches, until the children finally reached the Sky Dome at the very top of the school. School assemblies were always held in the Sky Dome, which had an incredible view of the City of Celestia. Ray would always look out at the Sun Citadel, which stood tall at the very centre of the city, with the big Sunflower in the sky at its point glowing brightly, providing the Earth with warmth and light during its daytimes.

But today, there was nothing but darkness. Ray felt a shiver run down her spine.

'This is bad, REALLY bad,' said Percy, tapping Ray's shoulder. 'You don't think this is –'

A HUGE bolt of purple lightning illuminated the skies, followed by the deepest rumble of

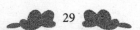

29

thunder. As another streak of lightning split the skies like spiky veins, the children gasped, and Ray felt as if her tummy had dropped into her toes.

In that moment of bright purple light, Ray couldn't quite believe what she was seeing. The pointy Sun Citadel building was gone, and so was the Sunflower that usually shone above it. Nothing was left apart from a large crater in the centre of the Forest of Fahrenheits, and a withered sunflower stem among the debris and destruction.

The students began muttering among themselves in panicked whispers. Some of them began running towards the exit.

'Students!' yelled Miss Glacielle. 'I don't want ANY of you leaving the Sky Dome! You *must* stay here where it's safe.'

'Miss Glacielle, I can help!' said Ray desperately. 'I know how to st—'

'Ray Grey,' said Miss Glacielle sternly. 'While under the Sky Academy roof, you are in MY care. And I cannot have anything happen to

you . . . Also, I really wouldn't want to face your mother if anything did.'

'This HAS to be Tornadia's doing!' Droplett growled and grabbed the edges of her rain cape angrily.

'Look, we don't know it's Tornadia for SURE,' said Snowden, trying very hard to stay calm.

Another fork of bright purple lightning tore through the skies, illuminating the great crater where the Sunflower used to be. This was followed by a familiar, ear-piercing, evil cackle.

Snowden blinked. 'OK, it's definitely Tornadia . . .'

Students screamed. Some were crying, some were running in circles and others were desperately trying to bypass the teachers to get out of the school.

Hundreds of snowballs splattered at their feet, making all the children jump to attention.

'We HAVE to remain calm,' said the head teacher firmly. 'Flailing around like tormented windsocks isn't going to help anybody, and it's certainly not going to solve this situation.' She took a deep breath. 'The other teachers and I will ensure your guardians know that you are safe. The entire Weatherlands is in lockdown, so your guardians will be safe too. If anybody needs the toilet, one of the teachers will chaperone you. Rest assured, the Weather Warriors and the Council of Forecasters will be dealing with this. They have been getting ready for Tornadia Twist to strike again so they are prepared.'

Despite her brave words, Ray couldn't help noticing a flicker of fear in Miss Glacielle's eyes.

'If Tornadia is here, then I HAVE to find out what my mystery gift is,' Ray whispered to her friends. 'Tornadia said she couldn't risk Rainbow Beard using his gift on her all those years ago. She seemed . . . afraid of it. This COULD mean that the gift, somehow, has a way to stop Tornadia from turning Earth into a storm planet and making herself Storm Queen!'

Snowden screwed up his nose. 'You're right, but, Ray . . . we've been searching for clues on this mystery gift for weeks now, and we haven't found *anything*. Even La Blaze couldn't . . .' He trailed off. 'Sorry . . .' Snowden knew how much Ray missed her friend.

'It's OK,' said Ray with a small smile. 'And you're right. I know La Blaze couldn't find out anything about Rainbow Beard's gift either. I just can't help feeling like we're missing something.'

Ray, Snowden and Droplett sat huddled together among the scared students and the anxious teachers. Gusty Gavin the librarian had set up a reading corner to help distract the children. A fourth-year lightning student used her beautiful magic to create little pink orbs to provide Gavin with light to read by. The other thunder 'n' lightning students banded together to create a circle of white lightning to illuminate the rest of the dome. Wind students used their instruments to blow calming tunes through the air, while a group of fifth-year snow students conjured ten large snowmen to stand guard by the windows and doors.

Ray's mind was spinning. She couldn't bear the thought of her dad and the other Weather Warriors out there fighting a battle that could potentially be solved if Ray discovered what her mystery gift was. She turned to Snowden and Droplett. 'I've had enough of waiting around. I'm going to the Rainburrow. Right now.'

CHAPTER 5
OUR LAST HOPE

'Ray, you can't just leave. It's too dangerous,' said Snowden, his face creased with worry. 'Especially for *you*.'

'I hate to agree with snow-boy,' said Droplett, 'but he's right. You're like Tornadia's arch nemesis. And while that sounds kinda cool, it's also VERY scary.'

'But I HAVE to find out what my mystery gift is!' urged Ray. 'It's our only hope . . .'

Snowden took Ray's hand. 'Then we're coming with you.' He raised an eyebrow. 'Besides, if Tornadia gets her way and takes over as Storm Queen, then she'll probably destroy the whole school, and we can't have that.'

Droplett put an arm around Ray's shoulders. 'You're gonna need someone particularly good at puddle-porting to sneak you out of here . . .' She winked.

37

'Tornadia is GOING DOWN!' said Ray. She got to her feet, braced her staff and swished her colourful hair dramatically, which just ended up flapping into her mouth.

'Even if we do stop Tornadia from becoming Storm Queen,' said Droplett, 'what do we do about the fact there's no SUN? The Earth and skies can't live without sunlight . . . That's one thing I do remember from General Weather Knowledge.'

'Clearly you didn't listen to the rest of that lesson,' said Snowden with a slightly smug smile. 'If you had, you'd know that the SunKeepers have millions of sunflowers growing in the Sunflower Fields.'

'But doesn't it take ages to fully grow a new sun?' asked Ray.

'Only from its seed form. Luckily the sunflowers in the field have all sprouted, so one of those wouldn't take too much time to grow into a fully sized sun at all.'

'I usually hate it when you're right,' said

38

Droplett. 'But in this instance, I'm really glad you are.'

There was a tap on Ray's shoulder, making her jump. She spun round to see Percy twiddling his fingers nervously and shuffling his feet. 'Ray, I'm scared,' he said softly.

'I know,' said Ray gently. 'But remember, I have something inside me that *could* stop Tornadia's evil plan . . . I just need to find out what it is.'

Percy nodded and the edges of his lips lifted a little. 'Your *secret* plan?'

'Exactly,' said Ray. She leaned in a little closer. 'But we need your help too. We need to sneak out of here without any of the teachers seeing. So, I was wondering if you might be able to cause a distraction?'

Percy bowed, looking much cheerier. 'Ray, I was BORN to distract.'

Without hesitation, he ran into the centre of the dome and shouted, 'ARRRGH, MY PANCREAS!' and fell to the floor.

39

'OK, I guess there's the distraction,' said Droplett, holding out one arm for Ray and Snowden to grab on to. Nim shrank to the size of a pea and tucked himself behind Ray's ear as he always did during a puddle-porting journey. As the students and teachers rushed over, Percy opened one eye and winked at Ray.

'Let's go to the Rainburrow!' said Ray, as Droplett swished her cape as hard as she could. Immediately, Ray felt herself drop into the puddle below. She should have been used to Droplett's puddle-porting by now, but something felt different this time. Since opening your eyes or mouth was a strict no-no during a puddle-port, Ray had no way of knowing why she felt an overwhelming sense of dread.

She squeezed Droplett's arm a little tighter, then found herself thrust sideways. Ray wasn't with Droplett any more. She opened her mouth to scream, but found herself swallowing water. Ray was knocked sideways again, her whole body sent spinning around and around. She could have sworn she saw another face watching her, the face stretched into an evil grin. Ray saw this mysterious Weatherling throw their arms forward, sending the puddle swirling in all directions, making Ray feel even more dizzy! Then it dawned on her that this Weatherling was a Rogue.

Ray felt herself spinning further and deeper into the infinite puddle portal. Droplett had always warned the friends to NEVER let go during a puddle-port, otherwise who knew where they might end up . . . Would Ray find a way out of this? Or would she be stuck in the puddles forever?

CHAPTER 6
PECULIAR PUDDLE

SPLOSH!

Something – *someone* – grabbed Ray's wrist. She found herself being dragged out of the water, coughing and spluttering. It took her a few moments to catch her breath.

'RAAAAY!' cried the familiar voices of Snowden and Droplett. Ray found herself hugging them so hard, never wanting to let go.

'Nim?' cried Ray, searching for the tiny cloud-cat behind her ear. 'Nim, are you OK?!'

There was a soft meow as the pea-sized cloud-creature plopped out of Ray's hair on to her lap. Nim slowly inflated back to normal cat size, then exploded.

'How above Earth did you manage to find and save me?' Ray asked her friends.

'Rain Weatherlings see puddles very differently to others,' explained Droplett. 'When I emerged with Snowden and saw you weren't there, I kept creating puddles around the area until I saw a bunch of colours . . . It's lucky you have rainbow hair, Ray!' she chuckled with relief.

'And I'm very lucky to have the best puddle-porter in the skies as one of my best friends!' said Ray, throwing her arms around Droplett once more.

'I'm sorry, Ray . . .' said Droplett, her voice cracking. 'But something is wrong with the puddle portals. I got disorientated and I was being thrown around like a pair of knickers in a tornado. I usually have complete control, but I don't know what happened. Nothing felt right.'

Ray was about to answer but coughed up a mouthful of rainwater and took a deep breath. 'Don't worry,' she continued. 'It wasn't your fault. There was a Rogue in there.'

'We should have guessed Tornadia would have an army of Rogues following her,' sighed

44

Snowden. 'I really don't think the Weatherlands are as prepared for her return as they think they are.'

Ray shook her head. 'Which is why we need to act FAST, and find out my mystery gift . . .' She got to her feet, but then realised they weren't in the Rainburrow.

'Where exactly did we puddle-port to?' asked Snowden, looking around them.

Ray squinted into the darkness. She tapped her staff twice on the soft ground illuminating the area with a halo of rainbow light.

'Dirt . . .' said Droplett. 'We're in a massive patch of dirt.'

'Wait,' said Ray, bending down. She scooped up a handful of the dusty ground in her palm and held her illuminated staff over it. 'It's sparkly dirt . . .'

'Sunflower soil!' said Snowden. He leaned over and sniffed at it once. 'Definitely sunflower soil. It smells like syrup.'

'If this is sunflower soil, then that must mean we're in the Sunflower Fields . . .' said Ray, a heavy feeling of dread in the pit of her tummy.

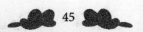
45

The friends were quiet for a moment. Ray took a few steps forward, pointing her staff towards the ground. 'If we're in the Sunflower Fields . . . then *where* are all the sunflowers?'

She held her staff a little higher, allowing the pool of rainbow light to expand. Withered stems and sizzled petals lay scattered across the ground. 'They've all been . . . destroyed,' Ray said, hardly able to believe what she was saying (or seeing).

'Does that mean . . . we have no suns left at all?' asked Droplett.

'It can't be,' said Snowden. 'The SunKeepers

have always made sure there were plenty of back-up sunflowers in case the worst happened.'

'I think the Sunflower Fields WERE the back-ups,' said Ray, anger building inside her. How DARE Tornadia do this to their incredible world?

Only the SunKeepers had the power to keep the Sunflower in the sky shining. Every Sun Weatherling was born and raised to become a SunKeeper. They attended a special sun school and once every eleven years, when the big Sunflower in the sky was due to reach the end of its shine, an Eclipse would commence and a

brand-new sunflower fully grown from the fields would replace the old one, along with five new SunKeepers to keep it glowing brightly.

But the last Eclipse had happened barely six months ago. And now that very Sunflower was gone, along with any hope of replacing it.

Ray's heart had never felt so heavy. She looked up towards the sky. As the Weatherlands were flooded in sunlight every day and night, they never usually saw the stars. But right now, the darkness meant that the night sky stretched as far as the eye could see. Tiny prickles of sparkling light twinkled above the friends. Even though seeing the stars was not great for the Weatherlands right now, Ray couldn't help feeling that this view was just what she needed. Then something caught her eye. One star shining brighter than all the rest.

'La Blaze,' Ray whispered and found herself smiling. She gripped her staff a little tighter, remembering La Blaze's last words to her before she died. 'Always be you . . .'

'Always be me,' Ray said to herself and

suddenly she felt a strength inside her she didn't know she had. 'I'm Rainbow Grey. And I NEVER give up.'

She turned to Snowden and Droplett, who were looking anxiously at her as she stared up at the sky muttering to herself.

'Come on,' said Ray. 'We're going to fix this. I'm bringing Tornadia down once and for all.'

Deciding not to chance puddle-porting again, Nim formed a big, fluffy cloud, and flew them back towards the Forest of Fahrenheits where Ray's special Rainburrow sat nestled below the Weatherstone Circle. Using an advanced snow spell, Snowden created an icy mirror around Nim – a handy trick to make them appear invisible. That way, the friends and Nim could avoid being spotted by any Weather Warriors.

As they flew away from the empty Sunflower Fields, Ray heard a loud SNAP from behind, followed by another SNAP SNAP SNAP!

Ray peered through Nim's cloudy barrier,

looking for where the sound had come from. Weather Warriors rushed through the skies in the direction of the Cloudimulus Suburbs.

Ray saw purple lightning strike the silver lining that had been holding the pod houses afloat, sizzling it away to nothing. Moments later the pod houses of the Cloudimulus Suburbs dropped from the clouds they'd been suspended from.

'NO!' cried Ray. 'What if my mum's at home? She has no magic to save herself. Nim, fly towards Cloud Nine, QUICK!'

Nim mewed and revved himself up, heading in the direction of the falling houses. Cloud Weatherlings were perched upon their cloud-creatures, flying to safety as their homes disappeared below them. Then Ray saw Cloud Nine, her home. A bolt of lightning stretched its way across the sky, scorching the cloud's silver lining, sending the house plummeting downwards.

CHAPTER 7
WHAT LIES BENEATH...

'NOOOOOOOOOOOOOOOOO!' Ray screamed, clawing her way out of the cloudy disguise of Nim's body.

'Ray! Wait! What if Tornadia sees you?' cried Snowden. 'She could be anywhere!'

'I HAVE TO SAVE MY MUM!' shouted Ray, balancing on Nim's cloudy tail, unable to think straight.

But then a familiar voice screamed; 'THAT ROGUE NEEDS TO FOG OFF! JUST WAIT 'TIL I GET MY HANDS ON HER.'

It was Ray's mum!

Ray spotted the grey-haired woman perched with Ray's dad on the back of Waldo the cloud-whale. As her parents whooshed past, not seeing the friends hidden by Snowden's clever ice-mirror spell, all Ray wanted to do was to check they were OK. What if her mum got hurt? But then a string of incredibly rude words carried through the gusts of wind. Something about 'using her best spatula to make Tornadia realise the true place the sun really didn't shine . . .'

'I think your mum is juuust fine,' said Droplett with a wink.

Ray chuckled, almost wanting to cry with relief.

Once again, lightning tore through the skies like a huge crack appearing on a china bowl. A boom of thunder had Ray and her friends covering their ears, before a swirling tornado ripped through the rest of the cloud houses, tossing them in the direction of the Flurry Mountains and the Valley of Winds. A high-pitched voice carried in the strong gales across the skies.

'YOU ALL KNOW WHAT I WANT!' cackled the evil voice of Tornadia Twist.

Ray felt a shiver run down her spine, followed by an overwhelming bubble of anger in her chest. 'Quick, Nim!' she urged, lowering herself back into the cloud-cat's disguise. 'We have to hurry to the Rainburrow!'

54

Somehow, even without there being any light, Ray knew when they'd reached the Weatherstone Circle as she felt a familiar tingle in her fingers and toes. At the Weatherstone Circle, six stones stood representing each type of weather, and in its very centre was a seventh: the Rainbow Weatherstone, standing tall and proud. Weather magic was at its strongest inside the circle.

Ray called out the password 'BEARD', to reveal the secret doorway into the Rainburrow. Ray and her friends launched themselves down the large rainbow slide which led deep underground.

What the friends hadn't expected to find at the bottom of the slide, illuminated by ambient lightning lamps, was a pigeon, lounging in a scented bubble bath.

'OH!' squealed Ray.

'MEOW!' squeaked Nim.

The pigeon in the bath looked up, seemingly not bothered by the new arrivals. 'Aren't you a bit

55

early for your afternoon rainbow gift practice?' he said, popping a bubble with a toe claw.

'Um . . . Coo La La, you have NO idea what's going on out there, do you?' Ray replied, unsure where to look.

'Although, I think the bigger question is where did that BATH come from?' asked Snowden. 'And how above Earth did a small pigeon like you get it down here?'

Coo La La raised an eyebrow. 'Soooo many questions,' he said casually. 'Can't you see

I'm trying to relax?' He began to get out of the bath.

'GAAAH! Try warning us before you expose YOUR PIGEON BUM!' Droplett bellowed, covering her face with her cape.

'In case you hadn't noticed, young Drip-Drop,' said Coo La La, ruffling his feathers, 'I'm a pigeon. I *never* wear clothes. My brilliant bottom is *always* exposed.'

Droplett was stunned into silence.

Coo La La had always stayed close to Ray's good friend La Blaze DeLight. (Although he would hasten to add he was *not* a sidekick.) But since La Blaze's death, Coo La La had become rather fond of Ray and her friends, even though he would never admit that.

'Seems the floating feline has found a new hobby,' said Coo La La, watching Nim spin slowly around in the air pawing at the bath bubbles.

But Ray had more important things to do. She began rummaging around the burrow sifting through her notes on rainbow weather magic.

The very notes La Blaze had spent many weeks organising for her.

'Are you going to tell me what's going on, or not?' said Coo La La nonchalantly, drying himself off with a tiny towel.

'The big Sunflower in the sky is gone,' Ray continued. 'Outside this burrow is just darkness and chaos. Tornadia is BACK.'

Coo La La put on his top hat and monocle then began to make himself a cup of tea. 'Well, that's not good,' he said casually.

'It's VERY bad and we really need to find out about my mystery gift,' urged Ray, rifling through a large cupboard in case there was anything there that she'd missed in a previous search for answers. Then she stopped dead as she spotted a shiny gold box with a sunflower painted on its lid.

'Did you find something?' asked Droplett, bounding over to Ray's side. Her expression drooped. 'Oh . . . Is that . . .?'

'My special La Blaze memory box,' said Ray with a small smile. She took a deep breath.

'All her special things are inside.'

Ray opened the lid gently, her chest tightening at the sight of the two sunflower wristbands, once used by La Blaze to channel her powerful sun magic. They still smelled of the nectar-sweet perfume she used to wear. Beside the wristbands was a small photo of La Blaze and Ray pulling silly faces in the Rainburrow, a silvery calling compass and a tiny, sparkling pouch.

'I wish you were here, La Blaze,' Ray whispered as she gently closed the box again. 'I miss you so much.'

Meanwhile, Snowden and Coo La La were arguing by the central tree stump. Nim was now in the bath.

'We could REALLY do with your help, Coo La La,' said Snowden in frustration.

Coo La La took a sip of Ozonian tea. 'You know, snow-boy. One can do a lot of thinking while having a bath,' he said.

'I'm sure one *can* but lounging in a bath doesn't help us to save the world,' said Snowden crossly. 'So, please help us search for some clues about Ray's mystery gift because outside of this burrow Tornadia is destroying everything!'

The pigeon put down his teacup. 'There *is* one thing I wanted to share, actually.'

Snowden leaned forward in anticipation.

'Why do you think that there's a tree stump *under* the ground?' Coo La La gestured towards the stump in the centre of the Rainburrow.

Snowden's left ear streamed with snowflakes. 'Is that it?' he said through gritted teeth.

'Actually, that IS really odd,' Ray chipped in. 'Since trees usually grow above ground.'

Droplett marched over and swiped the papers and rainbow notes off the stump, before stepping on top. She jumped up and down. 'Hear that?' she said. 'It's echoey . . . There's something under here!'

Ray's heart skipped a beat. 'Maybe it opens.

What if there's something inside?!'

Ray pulled at the stump before attempting to twist it, heaving and gasping as sweat trickled down her face while Coo La La watched.

'You could just try that latch there . . .' the pigeon said, pointing with his wing to a small metal object at the base of the stump, half buried in the roots.

'You could have SAID,' growled Ray.

'Coo La La . . . How long have you been pondering over this stump exactly?' asked Snowden.

'Probably a week,' Coo La La replied.

'Did you not think to tell us right away?' shrieked Droplett.

'I was *pondering*,' said Coo La La. 'Pondering takes time. I had to find the right moment.'

'You are one infuriating pigeon sometimes,' Snowden grumbled.

Coo La La flipped the latch at the base of the tree trunk, causing it to shift slightly.

The friends gasped and clambered forward,

using all their strength (again while Coo La La
watched) to slide the tree stump across the bumpy
ground.

And there, right in front of them, was a
secret tunnel.

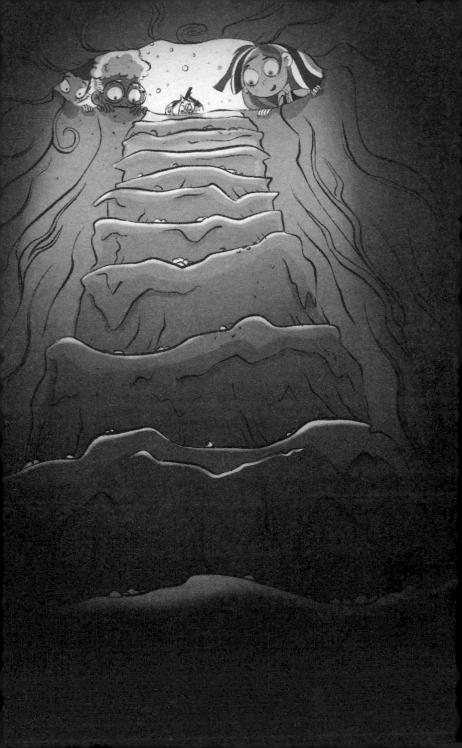

CHAPTER 8
DOWN, DOWN, DOWN...

Wibbly steps led all the way down into darkness.

'We don't have to go IN there . . . do we?' said Coo La La, taking a step backwards. 'It's UNDER the underground . . . that's way further down than I wish to go.'

'You wanted to be part of the gang,' said Ray kindly. 'That means sticking together, no matter what!'

Coo La La rolled his eyes. 'Ugh, fine. But we don't know how deep this is. What if we slip and FALL?'

Nim meowed merrily and squidged himself into the hole first. 'Meow!'

'Excellent idea, Nim!' said Ray with a grin. She turned to Coo La La. 'Nim will be our safety cushion.'

Coo La La opened his beak to speak then

sighed. 'I have run out of excuses.'

Ray lowered herself into the dark, vertical tunnel, gripping the root-covered walls as she carefully tiptoed her way down the narrow stairway. Coo La La made himself comfortable in Snowden's hair while the friends followed.

Nim meowed again as Ray found herself on flat ground. 'I think we've reached the bottom!' she called up towards the rest of the gang.

Ray felt her hands tingle furiously. More so than whenever she stepped into the Weatherstone Circle. She wiggled her fingers and shook her hands out, but the feeling wouldn't go away.

'We have touchdown,' came Droplett's voice.

Ray pulled her staff out from the back of her waistcoat and tapped it on the ground twice to activate Rainbow Light's gift. But it was impossible to see what lay ahead of them, even with the staff illuminated. There only seemed to be endless darkness.

'Well, this isn't scary at all,' said Coo La La sarcastically.

'It *is* a bit creepy,' said Snowden.

But Ray didn't feel scared or creeped out at all. She couldn't quite work out why, but something felt . . . right. Despite her heart beating hard as the world above fell apart, being here helped Ray to think clearer.

Ahead of them lightning crackled to life along the ground, revealing a long, arched tunnel lined with cascades of water. Tiny cloud-sheep danced on the ceiling. Nim was very happy about this and proceeded to try to eat one.

'Wow!' gasped the friends in unison.

'I was not expecting THAT,' said Droplett, gawping at the scene before them.

'This is incredible!' Snowden breathed.

'It's all right, I guess,' said Coo La La nonchalantly. 'If you like incredible, amazing, beautiful things . . .'

As the friends walked along the waterfall tunnel, Ray noticed images appearing in the water, as if moments in time had been captured in the shimmery cascades.

67

'I've read about these in an old book from the library called *Sky Stories: Myth or Fact*!' said Snowden excitably. 'They're called Waterfolios . . . created with advanced rain magic combined with rainbow weather magic. I've never seen any before, so naturally I thought they were just a myth!'

'Well, we all thought rainbow weather magic was a myth once upon a time,' said Ray, completely spellbound. She stared at the shimmery image before them.

A group of Rainbow Weatherlings stood side by side, wearing matching long-hooded waistcoats with beautifully embroidered rainbow weather symbols. Each Weatherling was holding a certificate. Behind this group were a set of older Weatherlings in long robes, including a long-bearded man Ray recognised as Rainbow Beard.

As they passed along the shimmering corridor, the friends gazed upon more sets of students holding their graduate certificates, watched over by proud teachers.

'We knew that Rainbow Beard was the head teacher of a rainbow school,' said Snowden as snowflakes poured from both ears. 'These must have been the students!'

Ray's mind was buzzing.

'That could've been you in one of those pictures if you were alive over a thousand years ago . . .' said Droplett with a wink.

'It could've been me *now* if Tornadia hadn't taken all the rainbow weather magic away.' Ray replied sadly as she followed more scenes of the rainbow graduates along the tunnel walls. She recognised a few of the teachers from pictures she'd found in the Rainburrow. But then Ray spotted someone that made her blood run cold.

'It can't be . . .' stammered Snowden.

'Duuuuude,' said Droplett with wide eyes.

'It's Rainbow Twist,' said Ray, feeling a familiar bubble of anger in her chest again. 'Before she became Tornadia Twist . . .'

Coo La La adjusted his monocle. 'Really?!' he said in a high-pitched tone. 'But she looks so . . .

friendly . . .' He frowned. 'She was a *teacher*?!'

'Yup,' said Ray. 'I read about that in a letter from Rainbow Beard. Then she turned into a villain.'

'Yeesh. She must've had a tough class that year,' said Coo La La, shaking his head sadly.

'Come on,' said Ray with a frown. 'We're not here to talk about what Tornadia used to be like.

We're here to stop what she's doing now.'

Ray and the friends walked further along the Waterfolio tunnel until they reached a big wooden doorway at the end. Ray pushed it open gently. Beyond was a large round room lined with shiny doors, each engraved with curly writing. A shimmering balcony ran around its top, and an extravagant-looking gold statue stood in the very centre. Ray recognised it immediately as a statue of Rainbow Beard. Her heart fluttered. 'THIS must be the ancient rainbow school! It's been here all along, right under our feet!'

'For somewhere that's been deserted for a thousand years, it sure is clean,' said Snowden.

Ray walked towards the shimmering statue of her ancestor. She lowered herself down next to Coo La La, who was studying his reflection in a bronze plaque. There were words engraved on the plaque, but Ray's mind was buzzing so much that the letters were getting terribly jumbled. 'What does that say?' she asked.

The pigeon flexed a wing and blew a kiss to his

reflection before reading aloud . . .

Together we stand, our gifts we give,
So skies and Earth together may live.
As long as Forever Crystals glow,
Storms shall pass, and peace shall flow.

PROFESSOR RAINBOW BEARD
of the Rainbow Academy

Ray felt a warm and fuzzy feeling run through her whole body. It was almost as if she'd heard these words before . . . like a lost memory being reignited. She looked up at the statue again. 'I wish Rainbow Beard was still here to explain this all to me,' she sighed.

'So, remind me, he's your great-great-great times how many grandad?' asked Coo La La, flying up to the statue's head. 'Hmm, I can't tell you how tempting it is to poop on this thing.'

'He's my great-great-great grandad times a LOT and please don't poop on him,' Ray replied.

72

'Ray, I thought you once said that your staff is the *very* staff that belonged to Rainbow Beard?' said Snowden as a snowflake popped out of his left nostril.

Ray twisted her staff around in her fingers. 'It is!'

'But if that's the case,' said Snowden, 'why does the staff in Rainbow Beard's hand look different?' He pointed towards the top of the statue where the professor stood proudly holding his staff high. Ray squinted her eyes and Droplett tilted her head to one side.

'There are two large, sparkly balls at the top of his staff . . .' said Droplett.

'You're right,' said Ray, feeling a little confused. She peered at the staff in her grip. 'This staff has two big circular holes.' She frowned. 'But this IS Rainbow Beard's staff . . . it has the word BEARD engraved in snow runes inside the top circle, look . . . ' She pointed to the tiny symbols, almost too tiny to see.

'Well, come on, you want to find out about

73

this mystery gift, let's hop to it!' said Coo La La, marching up to one of the many shiny doors. As he was about to push it open, the whole thing wafted away. 'That was NOT my fault,' he said defensively.

Ray touched the handle of another closed door, and immediately felt the weather magic flooding through her. The door exploded into thousands of tiny lightning sparkles, followed by a deep rumble of thunder, which made a little tune.

Droplett opened a door that changed colours every few seconds, and when Snowden went to explore another room, the door engulfed him in a bubble of water before transporting him inside.

Ray stepped through the sparkles into another large room. Desks formed a semicircle shape facing a larger desk piled high with books. A further enchanted waterfall cascaded from the wall behind the large desk. Ray tried her best to calm her racing heart and read the title of the book on top of the large pile.

'*Rules for Controlling the Magic of Others*,'

said a voice, making Ray jump.

'Coo La La! You could have TOLD me you were following me!' she squeaked, clutching her chest.

Ray flicked through the many pictures inside showing different Rainbow Weatherlings using their staff to control the magic of another Weatherling.

'I think this must be a classroom,' she muttered. It still felt so odd seeing illustrations all about rainbow weather magic! On the walls were

beautiful displays depicting the different types of weather, alongside handwritten quotes. Coo La La took it upon himself to read every single one.

'*The bond between the Earth and skies is the rainbow . . .*' he read aloud in a dramatic voice.

'*Don't just SEE the colours. Feel them. And most importantly HEAR them.*' Coo La La paused and frowned. 'Well, that's a load of nonsense. You can't HEAR a colour.' He rolled his eyes.

'And anyway, what about TASTE? No mention of –'

The pigeon's grumbles were cut short by the loud bellows of Snowden from one of the other rooms. 'RAAAAAAY! QUICK! I think you should see this . . .'

CHAPTER 9
IT'S ALL ... BLANK

Ray followed a trail of snowflakes that had been streaming from Snowden's ears, eventually stepping through a doorway labelled DORMS.

Ray and Coo La La found themselves faced with a whole new corridor lined with *more* doors. 'Through here,' said Snowden, popping his head out of a rainbow-coloured entrance further down.

Ray rushed inside to find a neatly arranged bed, some books, and a long waistcoat suspended in the air by wind magic beside a tall ice mirror.

'Look!' said Snowden, picking up a thick book from the bedside table. The title on the cover said: *A Record of Rainbow Gifts.*

'This could have answers about your mystery gift!' he said, passing the book to Ray.

Ray felt as if her heart might beat right out of her chest. She was grinning from ear to ear. This could be it . . . This could be the moment she FINALLY found out about her mystery gift. But as she flipped through the pages her expression fell.

'It's all . . . blank,' she said.

'Yikes, you're right,' said Droplett, peering at the plain, ragged pages.

'What's the point of a blank book?' cried Coo La La.

Ray thought hard. 'Think about it . . . the mystery gift was a secret among Rainbow Weatherlings. If there's top-secret information in there, they wouldn't have wanted others to see it . . . Especially if one of these books got into the wrong hands.'

'How above Earth do you read it then?' said Coo La La.

The friends stared at each other. Snowflakes poured from Snowden's ears. 'I have nothing . . .' he eventually said.

Ray dropped the book on to the bed and growled with frustration, letting her staff plonk down on to the pages. 'Why is everything so

 80

secretive?!' she cried.

'RAY!' Droplett squeaked. 'Look!' She was pointing towards the open book on the bed. The rainbow staff was still emanating a large halo of colours from using Rainbow Light's gift in the dark tunnel. And where the colourful beams met the pages of the book, words began to appear.

'Of course!' shrieked Snowden. 'It makes sense that only a Rainbow Weatherling's magic can reveal the information inside. The kind of magic no other Weatherling can do to keep the rainbow secrets hidden!'

'They didn't need to bother hiding it,' said Droplett squinting at the pages. 'The writing is ridiculously tiny.'

Ray peered at the teeny fancy letters emerging beneath the rainbow light. Then it dawned on Ray how many pages the book had . . . and Ray wasn't a quick reader at the best of times! 'There's no way I can read through ALL of that in time to stop Tornadia!'

'Don't worry.' Snowden smiled. 'Look!' He

81

turned the pages over one by one. 'This book is full of illustrations. Let's see if they might give us any clues. Remember, a picture can tell a thousand words.'

'Of course!' said Ray as the friends made their way through the magical pages. All the pictures were beautiful, but one caught Ray's attention. 'Stop!' she said suddenly. 'That one.' She pointed her rainbow magic towards an illustration of a Rainbow Weatherling standing proudly, holding their shiny staff upwards – just like the statue of Rainbow Beard in the entrance hall. The staff had two bright shiny crystals at the top. And the title of the chapter read: *The First Gift*.

The friends didn't waste any time. Nim reformed from his previous explosion as Snowden began to read:

In the beginning when the world needed it most, seven Weatherlings came together.

Sun, Snow, Cloud, Rain, Thunder, Lightning and Wind. They combined their powers to create a special kind of magic. Rainbow weather magic. The first born beneath the Eclipse amid the Weatherstones would receive this power.

Ameera Grey was the first born beneath the Eclipse and became the first ever Rainbow Weatherling. She could take control of all weather. But Ameera was also born with a special gift . . . the FIRST rainbow gift. The gift to bind *another's magic.*

From that day, Ameera became known as Rainbow Bind. This rainbow gift was passed down Ameera's family for generations.

This powerful gift was used for good. With the ability to bind the magic of Rogues who wished to put others in danger, Ameera's presence made the Weatherlings and the people of Earth feel safe. There was peace. There was balance.

But the Rogues felt threatened by this gift, by Ameera – the one Weatherling who could bind their magic and stop them once and for all. She became their prime target. If they could get rid of this rainbow gift then they were free to carry on using their magic for bad.

The Rogues would try everything they could to capture Ameera. From tornado traps to lightning cages to hurricanes with the power to sweep her right into space. But luckily Ameera fought her best fight against these Rogues, protecting the Earth and skies at all costs.

As years passed, it was decided that each child born as Rainbow Bind would be known to the rest of the weather world by a different name. Only the other Rainbow Weatherlings knew who the true Rainbow Bind really was. After all, it was far easier to bind a Rogue's magic if they didn't see it coming.

'Wow, the power to bind magic is HUGE!' said Snowden.

Ray paced the room, afraid that if she stopped moving, she might just explode like Nim!

'Rainbow Beard had to make up *his* name because his *true* gift couldn't be known by other Weatherlings . . . so the ability to bind weather magic must have been his gift . . .' She gasped. 'That means . . .'

'The power to bind must be the mystery gift!' the friends said in unison.

'Duuuuuuude. YOU have the power to take magic away?!' Droplett bellowed.

'That must be why Tornadia never wanted you to find out about it!' Snowden added.

'GUYS . . . if I'm part of the Rainbow Bind family line, that means I'm related to the FIRST Rainbow Weatherling that EVER existed,' cried Ray, 'and inside me is the first rainbow gift that ever existed!' Her mind felt like it had been turned inside out and upside down. It seemed absolutely incredible, but now it all made sense.

Droplett's rain cape was practically pouring, and Snowden's ears were fizzing with snowflakes.

'This is . . . This is . . . unbelievable!' cried Ray. I have the power to *bind* Tornadia's magic . . .' she shrieked as the realisation sunk in. 'I can take it away from her and actually *stop* her from destroying the Weatherlands and turning the Earth into a storm planet . . .'

Hope filled Ray's chest. She didn't know what to do or say in that moment, so she took Nim in her arms and spun around on the spot before tripping over her own feet and falling on to the bed. Even though her brain felt like it had exploded and been put back together again,

Ray stood up and braced her staff.

'I can and I WILL bind Tornadia's magic,' she said, feeling more determined than ever. 'I just need to learn HOW.' She pointed her staff towards the book to reveal the mass of tiny writing. 'Does it say anything in there?'

Snowden took a few moments to scan the text, his eyes disappearing further and further underneath his furrowed brows. He then paused. 'Wow . . .' he said, staring at the page.

'What does it say?' asked Ray eagerly. Her mind was a complete jumble of excitement, fear and confusion; it looked as if the letters were simply dancing around the page. She couldn't seem to focus on even ONE word.

Snowden read aloud:

The gift to Bind
The FIRST GIFT.
The original and most powerful.
A secret among Rainbow Weatherlings.

Never to be revealed outside the
rainbow clans.
In order to bind, one must possess the
Forever Crystals within their staff: the
Earth Crystal and the Sky Crystal.
Together they represent the Earth
and sky as ONE. We're all connected.
When binding – the Forever Crystals
will show you the way.

'Huh?' said Droplett, staring at the page.

'*In order to bind, one must possess the Forever Crystals within their staff* . . .' Ray recited. 'You were right earlier. My staff *is* meant to have two crystals at the top.'

Ray stared at the staff in her hand . . . the staff that definitely did NOT contain two crystals.

'Where above Earth *are* these Forever Crystals?' asked Droplett.

'I literally have no idea,' said Ray, 'but I have

to find them. They're the key to unlocking my binding gift.'

'Where do we even start?' said Coo La La. 'The crystals could be *anywhere*.'

Ray wracked her brains. After a few moments of silence she had a sudden thought. 'Guys, the Earth Crystal must have something to do with Earth, right?'

'That seems plausible,' said Coo La La.

'And who takes care of the planet?'

'Um . . . humans?' said Droplett and Snowden, looking unsure.

'Good grief, no,' said Coo La La.

'I'm talking about the Woodlings!' said Ray with a smile. 'I met a Woodling called Twiglett not too long ago. She was so kind and helpful.'

'Ooh, are the Woodlings the magical folk that live in the forests on Earth?' said Coo La La.

'Yes,' said Ray. 'And I'm sure they'll want to help us,' she said. 'Come on, let's go!'

'Wait!' said Droplett, grabbing the long waistcoat, which was floating in mid-air next to the long ice mirror in the corner of the dorm room. She made a loud squeal of joy, making Nim do a tiny cloud-wee on the floor. 'This is what the students are wearing in the Waterfolio tunnel!' She jumped up and down on the spot, sending splashes of rainwater over an unimpressed Coo La La. 'It's the Rainbow Academy uniform . . . Ray, YOU should wear it!'

'We should really go,' said Ray. 'If the Weatherlands survives then we can come back and explore this place properly.'

'But this is like your superhero moment, y'know, when the main character puts on their iconic costume in the last part of the adventure!' said Droplett, eyes wide.

'Wait a minute,' said Coo La La. 'If Ray puts it on, does that mean this is OUR last adventure? Are we ON an adventure?!'

But Droplett had already dressed Ray in the waistcoat before Ray could utter another word. 'Now you're guaranteed to win the battle for the skies!' She grinned and turned Ray around to face the icy mirror.

Ray's heart skipped a beat as she stared at the girl in front of her. Not just any girl. Rainbow Grey. Wearing this, she could imagine herself walking around this very school, chatting to fellow Rainbow Weatherlings. Being a real part of everything, not an outsider.

'It's like you were born to be a Rainbow Weatherling or something,' Droplett winked.

'Yes,' said Ray, feeling hope flood through her. 'And now it's time to find those Forever Crystals!'

CHAPTER 10

TINY TWINKLES OF DEATH

As Ray stepped out of the Rainburrow, she was greeted by a faceful of tiny, shiny specks.

'ARRRGH!' she coughed and flailed her hands around to waft whatever it was away.

'Are you OK, Ray?' said Snowden as the friends emerged behind her.

There was an almighty gust of wind throwing every one of them sideways and into the trees of the forest, narrowly missing the Weatherstones.

Ray landed smack bang in the middle of a patch of something very spiky. 'OUCH!' she cried, using her staff to help her clamber to her feet. It was still dark, but Ray knew the forest well enough to guess that she'd landed in a patch of prickly pinewafts. As she stepped away, she heard a *riiiip*. 'Well, I guess my new

93

Rainbow Academy waistcoat was never going to last for long . . .'

'RAY! WHERE ARE YOU?' shouted Droplett.

'Over here!' Ray called back. 'Look for my light!' She tapped her staff on the ground twice to activate Rainbow Light's gift. Nim meowed and appeared in front of her with his paws on his face. 'Oh, Nim,' said Ray. 'I'm so sorry you're having to go through this.' His paws moved slowly into the correct positions beneath his body and his lovely smile appeared . . . on his bottom.

Snowden and Droplett staggered over, followed by Coo La La, who was completely covered in Stenchamite Stalk goo.

'Don't even talk to me,' he said before another gust of glittering flecks flew straight into the pigeon and stuck to every single part of him.

'WATCH OUT!' Droplett screeched.

Ray turned to see something ferocious and sparkly tearing through the trees. 'Oh no . . .'

'GLITTER-NADO!' shrieked Snowden.

The themed tornado was Tornadia's speciality.

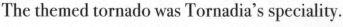
94

There were no limits to what the Rogue could turn into a swirling cyclone of death. Even the tamest of objects, such as a ball of cotton wool, had the ability to become the most destructive material in the world once combined with its fellow cotton-wool balls to create a squeaky, teeth-grinding, skin-crawling, nightmare whirlwind of misery, otherwise known as the cotton-wool-ball-nado.

A very glimmering Coo La La flew upwards as fast as he could into the treetops.

The friends threw themselves to the ground, and Nim expanded his whole body to protect them before getting aggressively splattered by tiny twinkles of death. But the force was too strong, and the cloud-cat exploded.

Ray covered her head with her arms. She could feel the showers of glitter thrashing against her body.

'WHO'D HAVE THOUGHT DANGER COULD BE SO PRETTY?!' squeaked Coo La La from above.

Finally, the wind died down and the friends

95

found themselves surrounded by a thick carpet of glitter. Ray could feel it in her nose, in her ears, between her toes . . . EVERYWHERE.

'That is THE worst kind of tornado!' growled Snowden, tilting his head to one side to allow a stream of glitter to fall out of his right ear.

The friends got to their feet slowly. Ray raised her illuminated staff, checking for any more signs of danger. Unexpectedly, a handbag went flying straight into Snowden's head, knocking him to the ground again. 'What the –'

'BAGS?' shrieked Droplett, ducking out of the way of a patched-up backpack.

As another tornado twisted and coiled through the trees of the forest, Ray could see that this one was going to be harder to avoid. It was FULL to the brim with bags of all shapes and sizes.

'THAT'S WHERE MY BEST PURSE WENT!' cried an angry Coo La La. He flapped his wings frantically, flying towards the bag-nado. 'I've been searching for it for YEARS.'

'No, Coo La La!' shouted Ray. 'Don't go any

closer! The bags are spinning too fast!'

But the pigeon needn't have worried about getting pummelled by his favourite bag, as a pair of frilly knickers swept him from the air instead.

'ARRRGH! Classic knicker-nado!' warned Ray as the swirling nightmare of underwear spiralled towards them.

Next to emerge was a hulking tornado FULL of rubbish. Ray wasn't sure what was worse . . . the smell or the fact that a very rotten globule of gale-force gruel had just lodged itself in her hair . . . A deadly crayon-nado zigzagged its way in front of the bin-nado, followed by a tornado full of bewildered Weatherlings called Bob, which Ray guessed was called a Bob-nado.

'MWAHAHAHAHAHAAAAAAAA!' The voice of Tornadia Twist carried through the winds.

After a rather unpleasant egg-nado had splattered its way past, the forest quietened down. Coo La La floated to the ground using a pair of knickers as a parachute. Snowden had at least five cracked eggs in his hair, and Ray was covered in colourful scribbles which she was pretty sure spelled out the word BUM over and over again. Droplett was frantically searching around the area in a panic.

'My rain cape!' she cried. 'It's GONE! It's been swept away by one of the tornadoes!'

Ray had never seen her friend look so worried before.

'I can't use my rain magic without my cape,' Droplett said frantically, still scrambling through the forest foliage. 'ARRRGH. It's too hard to search without the big Sunflower in the sky.'

'Try not to panic, Droplett,' said Snowden. 'We'll find it . . .'

'We don't have time to be searching around for a cape,' added Coo La La, echoing what Ray was thinking, but really didn't want to say.

'Without my cape, my rain magic will be harder to control . . .' cried Droplett. 'My magic could go wrong . . . it could go *rogue* . . .'

Ray grabbed Droplett's hands, the light of her illuminated staff making Ray's one purple eye and one blue eye sparkle. 'You forget . . . I'm a Rainbow Weatherling. I can take control of your rain magic and use it safely if we need it. You'll still be helping loads by lending me your magic.'

Droplett's face lit up. 'I guess you're right . . .'

The friends heard a CRACK of lightning and a deep grumble of thunder.

'Can't believe we've FINALLY met the legend that is Tornadia Twist,' said a sneery voice.

'Thunder 'n' Lightning Rogues!' hissed Ray. 'Quick! Hide!' She ushered the friends into the nearest Stenchamite patch, lowering herself as much as possible, to avoid anyone spotting her multicoloured hair.

'WELL, I CAN'T BELIEVE TORNADIA MANAGED TO BREAK US OUTTA PRECIPATORY PRISON,' replied the deep voice of another.

Ray, Snowden and Droplett gasped and looked at each other, eyes wide with fear and shock.

'*Tornadia's released all the prisoners*?!' squeaked Snowden.

'They'll regret leaving that lasagne behind,' sighed Coo La La wistfully.

'Come on, Bash,' said the sneery-sounding Lightning Rogue. 'We gotta find the last of the Council of Forecasters and put 'em in Tornadia's snot-nado.'

'I think I might be sick,' whispered Coo La La in response, trying not to gag.

'ONLY TORNADIA WOULD FINK OF A TORNADO AS 'ORRID AS THAT!' chuckled the Thunder Rogue called Bash.

'And ya should've seen the bogie-nado she

100

trapped those rotten SunKeepers inside,' said the Lightning Rogue. 'It's a work of art! The chaos is thrilling!' He erupted with a shrill laugh that would have fractured a glass window.

'These Rogues are horrendous,' said Coo La La, holding a wing to his beak. 'Snot. BOGIES? I don't even want to think about what else Tornadia might muster up!'

'Then let's NOT think about it,' said Droplett flatly.

'WE SHOULD 'URRY UP AND LOOK FOR THAT RAINBOW KID,' said Bash. His voice was getting quieter as they moved on. 'IMAGINE THE REWARD TORNADIA'LL GIVE US IF WE'RE THE ONE TO TRACK 'ER DOWN!'

There was a bright FLASH, forcing Ray to close her eyes before a rumble of thunder made it feel as if Ray's brain was a wobbling jelly inside her head.

'I can't believe the Council of Forecasters *and* the SunKeepers have been captured!' cried Snowden. 'Without the council, there is NO planned weather . . . Without SunKeepers, there's absolutely no hope of any sunshine ever again!'

'Calm down, boy,' Coo La La snapped. 'Let's try to look at the positive side of the situation . . .'

'Which is?' asked Snowden.

'It's Pitter Patter Pancake Day!' sang Coo La La. Snowden was about to reply with something rather unsavoury, but was cut short by the sound of footsteps approaching behind the friends, before a figure emerged from within the trees.

Ray thrust her staff towards the figure.

'WAIT! It's me!' cried a familiar-looking Weatherling as the light of the staff revealed their true identity.

'Mr Current?!' cried Ray as their bewildered teacher huffed and puffed his way into view.

'Children!' he wheezed. 'Thank the skies you're safe. I have been searching for you everywhere. We couldn't find you after . . .'
He took a few breaths.

'After what?' asked Ray desperately.

Mr Current looked at Ray with an expression

of concern she'd never
seen on a teacher's
face before. 'After
the Sky Academy
was destroyed by
an army of
ice giants.'

'WHAT?!'
cried the
friends in
unison.

'The *whole* school?!'
squeaked Snowden. 'Destroyed?'

Mr Current nodded sadly.

'Is everyone OK?' asked Ray, her heart
pounding.

'We had lots of Weather Warriors on the
scene, including your brilliant father, Ray,' said
Mr Current. 'And with the help of the teachers
we managed to get the children out using various
pieces of snow armour. Everyone was flown to the
Weatherstone Circle. We believe we will be safer

103

there where weather magic is strongest. You must go there too.'

'Nowhere is safe!' cried Ray. 'And I've found a way to stop Tornadia, so I'm going to Earth to find part of the answer.'

'You can't just go running off on your own with so many Rogues on the loose!' the teacher replied, but Nim had already expanded so that the friends could hop on to his back for flight. Coo La La tucked himself into Snowden's mop of hair, and the friends were OFF.

As the cloud-cat soared over the treetops, Ray heard the shouts and cries of Weatherlings all around. It was only when purple lightning lit up the sky that she truly saw the devastation.

Whole chunks of the Forest of Fahrenheits were simply gone as Weather Rogues

unleashed their chaotic power, tearing through the trees with vicious lightning bolts, or simply shattering them with almighty thunder claps. There were only a few cloud-houses left in the Cloudimulus Suburbs, and the Valley of Winds had been split in two. The crater in the centre of the City of Celestia where the Sun Citadel once stood looked like a huge abyss. Ray felt as if she were seeing everything in slow motion. Lightning flashed again, followed by the cold and menacing voice of Tornadia Twist.

'Raaaaaay Grey? Where are youuuuuuuu, Raaaaaay?' she oozed.

Ray felt the hair on her arms stand on end as Tornadia's voice pierced through her like an icy blade.

'Come out, come out, wherever you aaaaare!'

Ray shuddered and buried herself even lower into Nim's floofy body. Droplett squeezed her arm for reassurance, and Snowden had both gloved hands braced for any big snowball spells he might need to conjure up.

'Come out to plaaaaay, Raaaaay,' trilled Tornadia's tormenting tones. 'Just show us where you are, AND THIS CAN ALL BE OVER . . .'

'The real question is, where is SHE?' shrieked Coo La La. 'HOW is Tornadia everywhere yet *nowhere*?!'

'Just because we can hear her doesn't necessarily mean she's close,' said Ray shakily. 'Remember, voices carry on the wind.'

'And with an army of Rogue prisoners on her side, Tornadia will have ALL kinds of weather magic at her fingertips,' Snowden added.

'I'll bet any Rogue would fall head over heels to let someone like the infamous Tornadia use their power!' growled Droplett.

Another flash of Tornadia's purple electricity

tore through the heavens, illuminating more of the city below. Weatherlings were flying their wind instruments or running along snowy stepping stones, clutching their precious belongings and trying to dodge fierce ice-nadoes, fire-nadoes and even a spider-nado. Ray wasn't usually afraid of spiders, but when there were millions of them spiralling through the air, each with their eight legs flailing towards you, they suddenly became a whole lot scarier.

Then Ray spotted one of her favourite places – the Rising Bun Bakery. Well, what was left of it . . . The roof of the bakery was no longer intact, and instead of counters full of sizzling snowflake slices and rumblebuns, a huge puddle flooded the shop floor.

'I think I know why Slap and Streak didn't deliver the rest of the pitter patter pancakes . . .' said Droplett quietly.

'NOT THE BAKERY!' cried Coo La La. 'All those lovely cakes . . . WASTED.' He growled and curled his wings into fists.

'Destroying cakes is the *ultimate* crime.'

Piece by piece, Tornadia was destroying their world.

The largest snowball the kids had ever seen smashed into the Airy Apartments below, and a group of evil cloud-sheep were surrounding the hoard of dizzy Bobs who'd been thrust out of the Bob-nado. Tornadia's voice echoed through the squalls, sending a shiver down Ray's spine.

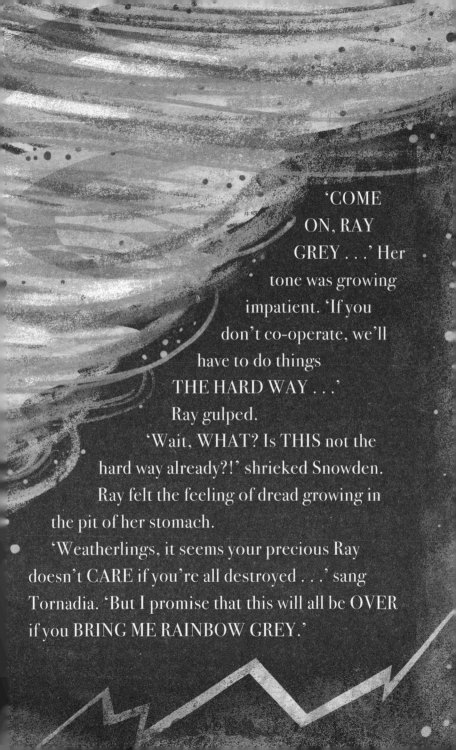

'COME ON, RAY GREY . . .' Her tone was growing impatient. 'If you don't co-operate, we'll have to do things THE HARD WAY . . .'

Ray gulped.

'Wait, WHAT? Is THIS not the hard way already?!' shrieked Snowden.

Ray felt the feeling of dread growing in the pit of her stomach.

'Weatherlings, it seems your precious Ray doesn't CARE if you're all destroyed . . .' sang Tornadia. 'But I promise that this will all be OVER if you BRING ME RAINBOW GREY.'

CHAPTER 11

FLY FASTER!

Every part of Ray wanted to burst out of her hiding place to confront Tornadia once and for all; to use every ounce of power she had to try to defeat the Rogue. But she knew that she couldn't. The only way to stop Tornadia was with her binding gift. And the only way to unlock that gift was to find the Forever Crystals.

Ray squeezed her staff in frustration. 'We HAVE to fly faster!' she urged. 'I won't let Tornadia destroy our home.' Her heart was beating furiously, and rainbow weather magic pulsed through her body. She knew that without her staff, her magic would be MUCH, MUCH stronger – perhaps even strong enough to give Tornadia a run for her money . . . But without the staff, Ray's magic would also be more dangerous, and she'd be putting everyone and everything around her at risk. Ray took a deep, calming breath. 'I will stop Tornadia . . .' she muttered to herself. 'And I will stop her by doing what is right. What is GOOD.'

Out of nowhere a bright red bolt of spiky electricity narrowly missed Nim's whiskers, sending the cloud-cat spinning into an explosion.

The friends screamed as they plummeted towards the ground. Another lightning bolt almost sent the illuminated rainbow staff flying from Ray's grip.

Coo La La was flapping frantically against the wind, spinning in circles and squawking loudly, while Snowden was desperately trying to draw a snowflake in the air to save the friends from their flattened fate. But the white flakes kept getting swept away in the hurricane winds.

Ray felt a sliver of panic cut through her as she lost the ability to focus, spinning around and around. She felt motion sick and braced herself for the impact of the ground any second now.

But at the last minute Droplett threw out both

112

hands, using her rain magic to create the most almighty splurge of rain. It soared through the air towards the friends, engulfing them just before they hit the ground. The water bubble bounced to a stop and then exploded with a great big SPLOSH, soaking them all.

'Even when it's the end of the world, I get sploshed,' sighed Snowden.

'Please don't tell anyone I used my magic without a cape,' Droplett said quickly. 'It was either use Rogue magic or *die* . . . And, well, I didn't fancy us dying.' She was speaking at a windillion miles per hour, a bead of sweat running down her temple. 'But trust me, I won't use that kind of magic EVER again. It felt as if I might flood the sky!' She shook out both hands and danced on the spot as if grossed out by something.

'Well, for a first-time Rogue, you didn't do too bad,' winked Ray. 'You saved us all from becoming Pitter Patter Pancakes!'

'Where are we?' said Snowden. Ray held her staff in the air to get a better spread of rainbow

113

light over the surrounding area.

'I think this is Crackle Corner,' she said quietly. 'Although it looks more like a heap of debris now . . .' The place was unrecognisable. Once a beautiful cobbled area with a large water fountain at its centre and tiny weather shops dotted around in a higgledy-piggledy fashion, Crackle Corner was now a pile of broken stones, squashed cakes and fallen debris from all over the city.

Coo La La swooped down to the ground, tapping the top of his bare head angrily.

'WHO TRIED TO STRIKE US WITH LIGHTNING?!' he shrieked. 'BECAUSE THEY OWE ME A NEW TOP HAT.'

'It must have been one of Tornadia's Rogues,' said Ray, looking around for signs of anyone lurking nearby.

Nim began to reform, looking a little worse for wear. He purred sadly as his whiskers sprouted in place of his legs. 'Oh, Nim,' said Ray, hugging the half-formed cloud-cat. 'That wasn't your fault.

Are you OK to fly?'

Finally the rest of Nim's limbs reappeared but in all the wrong places, making him look more like a mutant cloud-centipede, but he smiled anyway and expanded for flight.

'Come on, we must hurry to Earth as fast as we can!' said Ray, about to swing herself on to Nim's back (or it could have been his belly . . . it was hard to tell). But another zap of lightning ricocheted off the cobbled ground not far from Coo La La, making the pigeon yelp and sneeze and fart all at the same time.

'Oh no no. I don't think so . . .' said a thick voice. 'It's time for Rainbow Grey to GO . . .'

'There's only TWO horrid Weatherlings I know who annoyingly rhyme like that every time they speak,' whispered Droplett.

'Frazzle and Fump,' said Ray darkly.

'You don't think Frazzle and Fump are gonna turn you in, do you?!' squeaked Snowden. 'I know they're awful, but I didn't think they were *that* cruel . . .'

Another rod of electricity rocketed through the darkness. The city square was illuminated in a ferocious red light long enough for Ray to spot an ALMIGHTY swirling puddle just a few metres away from them. It didn't look like a very friendly puddle . . . and the evil cackles from within it certainly didn't make it SOUND like a very friendly puddle.

'Guys, be careful –' Ray began, but another lightning strike sent Snowden and Droplett catapulting towards the puddle trap.

Ray threw her staff to the ground and grabbed both of their hands just before they disappeared into the water. But she had severely underestimated how heavy trying to drag two eleven-year-old Weatherlings out of a puddle trap would be.

'THIS IS A ROGUE PUDDLE!' cried Droplett.

'I can feel it sucking us in!' shrieked Snowden.

Ray could see the puddle churning as it

dragged her friends inside its watery void.

'I WON'T let go!' she shouted, trying to ignore the fact that her arms felt like they might pop out of their sockets.

Coo La La ran over and poorly attempted to pull Snowden out by his hair, instead successfully pulling out a clump of white curls.

'OUCH! THAT IS NOT HELPING!' Snowden yelled.

'I'm sorry but last time I checked, YOU WERE ROUGHLY ONE HUNDRED AND SEVEN POINT FOUR TIMES THE AVERAGE WEIGHT OF A PIGEON!' Coo La La shrieked, throwing the clump of hair into the spinning puddle trap.

'WHEN DID YOU GET SO GOOD AT CLOUDULATIONS?!' cried Snowden.

'I might be the most beautiful pigeon in the skies, but I also have a Sky–Q of one hundred and ninety-five!'

'YOU ARE PROFOUNDLY GIFTED!' Snowden exclaimed.

'Um, GUYS,' shouted Droplett. 'Save it for when we're not about to be sucked into an EVIL PUDDLE OF DEATH, OK?!'

A bright red light floodlit Crackle Corner, revealing a tall Lightning Weatherling with long black hair almost touching the floor. There was a red streak running through it.

'That's not your fellow enemy Frazzle, is it?' squeaked Coo La La. 'Unless this war has aged her by thirty years?!'

'Billowing breezes, I think that's Frazzle and Fump's mum . . .' said Ray, making the connection.

'She's meant to be in Precipatory Prison!' said Coo La La. 'I know that for a fact because she was in the cell next to mine during my BRIEF visit . . .'

'Well, she's obviously NOT in prison any more!' squeaked Ray, gripping her friends' hands a little tighter.

'*This is the most pathetic thing I've seen . . .*' the Lightning Rogue sneered as she waltzed towards the friends. '*Your power will be taken, and Tornadia WILL be our queen!*'

'Sizzling snowflakes,' said Snowden, 'I see where the twins get their rhyming habits from.'

The Rogue tilted her head to one side and grinned.

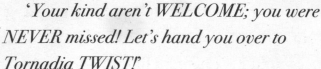

'*Your kind aren't WELCOME; you were NEVER missed! Let's hand you over to Tornadia TWIST!*'

'Ray, you have to save yourself!' gurgled Snowden, his nose barely above the waterline. 'Let go of us and grab your staff!'

'No! I'm not leaving you!' cried Ray.

Nim wrapped himself around Ray's belly and began to fly in the opposite direction in an attempt help her drag Snowden and Droplett to safety. But it was no good.

Poor Nim ended up over-stretching and exploding once again.

'Just . . . hold . . . on!' said Ray, her voice strained as she tried to keep her grip. But her arms were sore, the puddle was too strong and Frazzle and Fump's evil mother was conjuring a rather suspicious-looking lightning net.

'RAY, YOU HAVE TO LET GO!' yelled Droplett, trying to wiggle her arm free from Ray's grasp. Both of the friends were almost completely submerged now. But Ray didn't let go. She wouldn't let go. She *wouldn't* give up on them!

The Lightning Rogue stepped forward, spinning her electric net above her head. Ray could feel the electricity getting closer, making her multicoloured hair stand up on end. But before the net could make contact, an almighty rumble of thunder shook the ground. Then a long thin streak of green electricity surged through the lightning net, breaking it into thousands of crackling pieces.

Ray looked up to see the last two Weatherlings

she'd expected to see standing on the opposite side of the puddle trap. Frazzle and Fump Striker. They marched straight towards their mother.

'*STOP! Leave them alone!*' said Frazzle, her eyes glowing bright green with anger.

Fump stepped forward. '*Ray is just trying to save our home!*'

'*You must think I'm some kind of FOOL,*' their mother spat at them. '*I should never have sent you both to that school!*' She conjured another lightning net. '*You've always been cowardly, puny and WEAK. Step aside, little Strikers – I'm taking the FREAK!*'

But Frazzle and Fump combined their weather magic: lightning stick and thunder drum perfectly in sync. Flicking her lightning stick in sequenced directions, Frazzle sent her own VERY large lightning web towards her mother, before Fump bashed his thunder drum, directing a shockwave through the air. Their Rogue mother, now trapped within her own daughter's electrical web of lightning, went soaring straight into the puddle trap with an almighty **SPLOSH**.

Frazzle and Fump ran over to Ray's side. Only Snowden and Droplett's hands were visible now, as the puddle sucked them in further. The Striker twins helped Ray to drag Snowden and Droplett to safety.

It took a few moments for the children to catch their breath. Ray picked up her staff – it was still illuminated by Rainbow Light's gift – and stared at the twins in disbelief.

'Guys . . . you . . . you helped us . . .' she stammered. 'Thank you!'

'That felt really good . . .' said Frazzle with a big smile.

Ray waited for Fump's rhyming reply.

But then he finally said, 'We've never been proud of our muvva.'

'HOLD ON a puff-pod-picking minute!' said Droplett. 'You didn't rhyme with your sister?!'

The twins looked at each other and grinned.

'We finally did it, Fump,' said Frazzle. 'We stood up to Mum and now we can move on . . .' The Striker twins helped a rather speechless Ray to her feet.

'Now GO,' said Frazzle urgently. 'Save the Earth and Skies!'

CHAPTER 12
TO EARTH!

'What JUST HAPPENED?!' shrieked Droplett as Nim flew at super speed through the darkness. 'Frazzle and Fump?! Helping? Being nice? Not rhyming?!'

'It was the pancakes, wasn't it?' said Snowden, trying to get his head around the whole situation. 'All it took for them to be nice to us was sharing some *pancakes*?!'

'We can digest that development later,' said Ray, remembering the state of the city below with a shudder. 'We have to hurry!'

Ray's heart beat faster and faster as the gang headed towards the darkened Earth. It was beyond horrendous to see the planet swamped in shadow. 'We need to head for the Biggest Forest in the World,' she breathed. 'The Woodlings should be there.'

'But how will we find it without a map, in complete darkness?' asked Droplett, holding Ray's waist tightly as Nim soared through the cold air.

Ray hesitated. She hadn't actually thought about that!

'Don't worry,' said Snowden. 'I know the way. I like to memorise Earth maps in my free time.'

'I will not respond with something sarcastic. I will not respond with something sarcastic. I will NOT respond with something sarcastic . . .' muttered Droplett. Snowden poked his tongue out at her.

Ray smiled, thankful for her brilliant friends. They made this terrifying and uncertain misadventure seem a little less scary and a LOT more hopeful.

They were within Earth's atmosphere now. Ray could see flashes in the distance as storms raged across the world, and the glowing red eyes of evil cloud-creatures lurking in the skies.

'We need to be at least five degrees to the east

128

now . . .' said Snowden.

'You know,' said Coo La La, shuffling up to Snowden's side. 'Our brains together could do GREAT things.'

Snowden smiled. 'I'm sure they could.'

Millions of twinkling specks dotted the dark land below as if a whole constellation of stars rested upon the Earth. Lamps were switched on inside homes and offices. As pretty as it looked, Ray knew this was BAD. It was meant to be daytime on this side of the Earth.

As they flew closer to the planet, the wind began to pick up. Nim was flung sideways in a huge blast of air, followed by the loudest ROAR of thunder. There were screams from the humans below as lightning orbs chased them through the streets, into their homes.

'The Rogues are out in full force!' shrieked Droplett.

Ray leaned forward, urging Nim to fly faster towards the Biggest Forest in the World, guided by Snowden's directions.

129

They passed aeroplanes flashing red and green, trying to find a safe place to land. Confused birds struggled against the gale-force winds that carried them for miles and miles.

'HERE!' Snowden suddenly said, pointing downwards.

Using her staff to light the way ahead, Ray guided Nim towards the treetops, hoping against all hope he would reach the ground before exploding. 'YOU CAN DO IT, NIM!' yelled Ray as the cloud-cat pushed through torrential rain and icy blizzards.

POOF!

Nim exploded a few feet away from the ground.

Coo La La screamed as the friends fell to their bottoms with a DONK.

'Funny how the only one of us screaming is the only one who has WINGS,' said Snowden, giving Coo La La a yes-I'm-talking-about-you kind of look.

'No squabbling now,' said Ray, peering around at the thick tree trunks intertwined with ivy and various climbing plants. 'We have Woodlings to find, Forever Crystals to find, a world to save and a Rogue to BIND.'

'How do we know if the Woodlings are still here?' asked Droplett. 'They're probably hiding from all the storms!'

As the rain battered their heads, and the temperature dropped severely, the friends stepped between curly plants wilting beneath the icy frost and hissing creatures slithering through the undergrowth to find somewhere warm to hide. Even though Ray couldn't see anything apart from the patch of forest illuminated by her staff, she could FEEL the hundreds of forest animals around them.

'What if we're looking in the wrong forest?!' said Coo La La.

'Woodlings are a part of ALL forests,' said Snowden. 'I read that in a book called *The Forests of Earth; Forest Magic unveiled.*'

'Keep your ears and eyes open for any sign of movement among the trees . . .' said Ray.

There was a BOSH as Snowden tripped over.

'I HEAR SOMETHING,' shrieked Coo La La.

'It was just me,' groaned Snowden. 'Think I must have got my foot caught on a tree root.'

'No, actually, that was my foot,' said a voice. Ray pointed her staff towards where it had come from. What looked like a wiggly tree root moved and became the leg of a small creature. It stood slowly to reveal the rest of its body. From the light of her staff, Ray could see that the creature had vivid green skin and bright magenta eyes. There was a shuffle of leaves and whispers from above. Among the canopy of the forest, more glowing magenta eyes began to flicker into view.

'It's the Woodlings!' gasped Ray with relief.

'We've met before!' said one of the smaller Woodlings, skipping forward into the staff's light. She pointed up at Ray. 'You're *Rainbow Grey*!'

Ray recognised the tiny Woodling. 'You're Twiglett! Hello again.'

The small creature weaved her hands around in the air, creating glittery green sparkles, which eventually turned into a large leaf to shelter the friends from the rain. Then the Woodling waved to Snowden, Droplett and a very wet Coo La La.

An even smaller Woodling trundled up beside her with a huge mop of curly blonde hair. She pointed at Ray and blushed before burying her face in Twiglett's belly. Twiglett chuckled. 'This is my sister, Budlett. I've told her all about you, Ray, so she's a little rainbow-struck.'

One by one, more tiny Woodlings began to surround the friends, creating more leaf canopies with their magic. They walked on tippy-toes, treading with utmost care as they crossed the flowers and moss that carpeted the bumpy forest floor.

Twiglett took Ray's hand gently. Ray felt the Woodling's forest magic lightly tickle her skin. But the creature looked concerned. 'Do you know where the sunshine has gone?' she asked.

Ray felt sick having to tell them the truth.

'Tornadia Twist has destroyed our sun.' There was a resounding gasp from all the tiny forest creatures. 'She is destroying the Weatherlands as we speak, but we might be able to stop her,' she said. 'First I need to find something very important. Can you help me?'

The crowd of tiny creatures began to part. There was a shuffling sound before an ancient Woodling stepped into the staff's light. She was hunched over and had too many wrinkles to count, with vines intertwined with her limbs as if they were a part of her. She held a long wooden stick covered in straggly long tendrils and leaves.

'Ray, Snowden, Droplett . . . Coo La La . . .' she said in a croaky voice.

'How do you know our names?' asked Ray in surprise.

'Everybody knows MY name,' Coo La La muttered.

'I know the very fibres of this Earth. Everyone and everything that steps on to this planet,' said the old Woodling. 'I am Mother Root.'

CHAPTER 13

MOTHER ROOT

'Sizzling snowflakes, you're THE Mother Root?!' squeaked Droplett. 'We were told stories about you at Trickle Towers orphanage!

Nim floated up to Mother Root, meowed sweetly and morphed into a flower. Ray had never seen him do that before.

'We really need your help, Mother Root,' said Ray, stepping forward. She told Mother Root everything as quickly as she could. The tiny Woodlings flinched every time Tornadia's name was spoken.

Mother Root sat herself down on a mossy mound. 'I was beginning to believe the Forever Crystals were *forever forgotten*,' said Mother Root with a sad smile. 'Before the Rainbow Weatherlings disappeared a thousand years ago, those crystals were the very heart of our existence.

Representing the Earth and skies . . . Human and Weatherling . . . as one.'

'It seems the crystals were a part of Rainbow Beard's staff . . . the very staff I have here,' said Ray, holding out the long, golden instrument.

'Oh, it's sooooo shiny!' gasped Twiglett.

'You're lucky you found the staff *at all* after so many years,' said Mother Root looking a little surprised. 'But that staff without the Forever Crystals is . . .' She paused. '. . . like a Weatherling without a heart and brain.'

'Eww,' said Coo La La.

Mother Root got to her feet. 'Our hearts and brains work together as one and so do the crystals,' she said as she began to walk away through the trees, elegantly dodging large icicles falling to the ground with a SMASH. Ray followed close behind.

'Together the crystals channel unbelievable magic through the rainbow staff,' Mother Root continued, 'giving you the ability to eliminate a storm from its very roots.'

'The ability to *bind* weather magic,' said Ray, still hardly able to believe SHE had this gift somewhere inside her.

'What makes the crystals so powerful?' asked Snowden.

'The Earth Crystal was made by the very first Woodling using a very special substance from our trees,' said Mother Root. 'And the Sky Crystal was created by the very first Rainbow Weatherling by combining every type of weather into one. Together, the two crystals created the bond between the Earth and skies, giving their owner the ability to bind another's magic. But when Tornadia Twist robbed the Rainbow Weatherlings of their precious magic and created the one-hundred-year-old storm, the Forever Crystals were lost.'

But Ray was focusing on Mother Root. Something about her expression told Ray that there was more.

The old Woodling headed deeper into the dark forest. Ray noticed the tiny green sparkles

139

bouncing off the creature's skin. The leaves above rustled violently in the strong winds, before Coo La La narrowly missed getting hit on the head by a large hailstone.

Mother Root finally stopped by a bobbly tree, covered in mushrooms of all sizes and colours.

'I spent many, many years trying to put things right,' she continued. 'Even on the coldest days and the hottest seasons, I didn't give up hope . . . Using every ounce of my knowledge of forest magic, I created a *new* Earth Crystal.'

Ray bounced up and down on the spot. 'YOU HAVE AN EARTH CRYSTAL?! Where?!' she shouted.

'Careful now,' said Mother Root, suddenly looking serious. 'Only a Weatherling worthy of the Earth Crystal can make contact with it . . .' She gestured to the bobbly mushroom tree next to them.

'What do you mean?' asked Ray, suddenly feeling very nervous. Was she worthy?

'If you are truly a descendant of the Bind

family, then you have
nothing to fear . . .'

'Ray IS a descendant
of Rainbow Beard,' said
Snowden firmly. 'HE
was a Rainbow Bind . . .
Ray HAS to be the true
bearer of the Forever Crystals,
otherwise . . . otherwise I'll eat
my glove!'

Droplett leaned in towards
Ray. 'Please be the true bearer
because Snowden digesting a glove
is NOT something any of us wish to
experience . . .'

Ray felt an unwelcome trickle
of doubt run through her veins.
What if somehow she WASN'T
a descendant of Rainbow
Bind? What if somehow this
was all a big mistake?

Then she took a deep

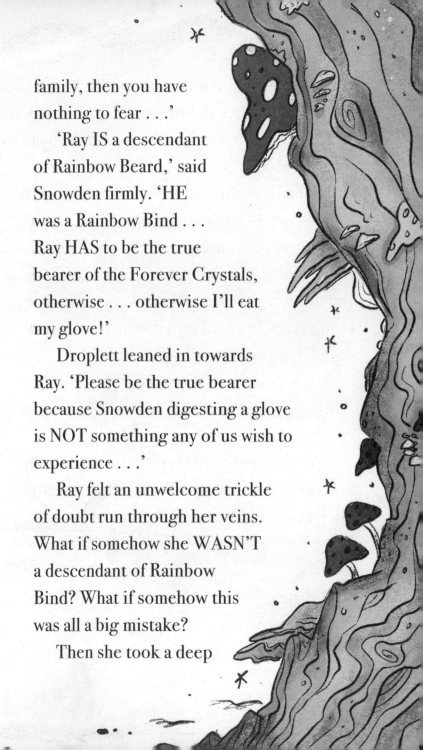

breath and looked at Mother Root. She nodded once. 'This is our last hope . . . If I'm the true descendant then this will bring us one step closer to saving our Earth and skies. And if I'm not . . .' She gulped. 'I guess I'll find out.'

She felt Snowden squeeze her hand. Ray smiled. 'Don't worry . . . this isn't half as scary as playing with forbidden magic.' She winked.

Snowden gave a half laugh, half sob.

'I'm ready,' said Ray, looking at the bobbly tree.

Mother Root touched the tree trunk lightly. Where her hand lay on the bark, it seemingly turned to liquid before revealing a small hole. Ray gasped as something inside the hole began to wildly glow bright green.

'If this Earth Crystal truly belongs to you, then it is yours,' said Mother Root, stepping out of the way for Ray. She gestured to the tree.

'You're not putting your hand in the scary glowing tree, are you?!' said Coo La La, tugging at the ends of Ray's hair. 'What if it EATS you?!'

Ray stepped towards the tree trunk. She felt a tingle on her skin, as if something were activating her magic, before she reached towards the green glow.

Her hand was burning, but it wasn't unpleasant. Was she doing the right thing? If she wasn't the true descendant then who knew WHAT would happen to her, plus she'd lose any chance of saving ANYONE and ANYTHING. But on the flip side, if she *were* (which she truly believed) then she had a chance to save everything. Without another thought, Ray closed her fingers around the green glow, feeling the crystal in the palm of her hand before everything went dark.

Ray felt dizzy. She blinked a few times. Everything was pitch-black. But she wasn't scared. She felt calm. She felt loved. Then, in front of her eyes, unknown Weatherlings appeared. Each of them had multicoloured hair, one blue and one purple eye, and each was holding a winged staff bearing two bright crystals. Soon Ray spotted a familiar face. Rainbow Beard!

The figures that appeared after Rainbow Beard suddenly had grey hair and did not carry a staff. But they had the same eyes.

Then Ray saw her own mum, Cloudia Grey, looking more brilliant and beautiful than ever. Ray was overcome with love. 'Our magic is yours,' said a voice. It was, Ray realised, her family line since the very beginning of the Rainbow

Weatherlings. Each one, a true Rainbow Bind . . . and Ray was the next.

The next Rainbow Bind. SHE was worthy.

Ray blinked again and found herself back in the forest with Mother Root and the other Woodlings. The creatures gave a little cry of joy as the roots around their feet began to glow. Then Ray herself began to glow! Mother Root bowed her head. 'In our darkest days, a new light has been born. You, Rainbow Grey, are a true Rainbow Bind.'

CHAPTER 14

GLIMMER

Nim meowed with joy and morphed into another beautiful flower shape. Snowden and Droplett sighed a HUGE sigh of relief.

'I can't believe I'm holding the Earth Crystal,' Ray muttered as she turned the shimmery object over in her palm.

There was a sob. Coo La La sniffed. 'I'm sorry, it's just the new waistcoat and the staff and the crystal and –' He waved his wing up and down at Ray. 'You've grown up so fast.'

Ray stared at the crystal in awe.

'The Earth Crystal can ONLY be created with *pure* Glimmer,' said Mother Root. 'I am the only Woodling who can collect this very special essence. I've been gathering Glimmer over the past one thousand years in the hope that one day it might be of use once again.'

'Hold on,' Coo La La cut in. 'Are you over a thousand years old?'

Mother Root dabbed at her cheeks and winked. 'Dear Coo La La, I'm as old as the Earth itself.'

'You, ma'am, are positively radiant,' said the pigeon. 'If the world doesn't end, then I'll be back to take notes on your daily facial routine.'

'What *is* this Glimmer exactly?' asked Ray, staring at the magical green object.

Mother Root held on to her walking stick with both hands. 'Every tree has a soul,' she said. 'The trees *love* the weather, and they feel joy when the weather is good. When trees are happy, they release a special kind of essence. An essence of hope . . . called the Glimmer.'

'Is it like the opposite of Shadow Essence?' asked Droplett.

Mother Root nodded. 'Have you ever noticed you feel happier after a walk among the trees, whether that be on Earth or in the Weatherlands?'

Ray nodded.

148

'The more Glimmer is released, the happier it makes those around it,' Mother Root continued. 'But like you or I, a tree also feels pain. When a tree is cut down before the end of its life, the Glimmer turns into deep, dark Shadow Essence.'

The other Woodlings recoiled. The mere thought of a tree feeling hurt upset Ray.

'That's why Shadow Essence consumes rainbow weather magic,' Mother Root said sadly. 'It's the pure pain and anger of the Earth, simply searching for any ounce of light and joy.'

Ray squeezed the Earth Crystal tightly. But then she suddenly felt a little light-headed and stumbled backwards.

'The Glimmer,' said Mother Root helping Ray to keep her balance. 'It enhances your rainbow gifts . . . but because you have so many gifts inside you, it's probably going to take a bit of getting used to. But if anyone can embrace the power of Earth magic, then it's you, young Rainbow Grey.'

Ray felt the warmth of the Earth Crystal in her palm. She slotted the round green gem in the bottom ring of her staff. It fitted perfectly. It was only then that Ray realised how bare the staff had looked without it.

Mother Root placed a hand gently on Ray's arm. 'Go now. I have faith in you, Rainbow Grey.'

'Thank you for your help, Mother Root!' said Ray as Nim rubbed himself against the old Woodling's ankles.

Mother Root bowed her head. 'You are the one who will reconnect our land and your skies. YOU can make them one again. And with the Earth Crystal, you are one step closer to becoming the most powerful Rainbow Weatherling.'

With a blink of an eye, the Woodlings disappeared into the foliage, becoming part of the forest once again.

Ray was feeling very positive until she spotted the big hole in her staff where the Sky Crystal was meant to be. And the huge hailstones that began plummeting to the ground around them.

'ROOOOGUE!' cried Ray, covering her head with her arms. The hail was HUGE. The size of geese. Then Ray realised there *were* geese falling to the ground.

'We have to get out of here!' shouted Snowden.

The friends began running through the trees, careful not to trip over large, wiggly roots or step on tiny, hidden creatures. Ray found it hard to run and hold her rainbow staff steady to help guide their way with the rainbow light. The wind picked up, pushing the friends backwards, and just as the hail-geese stopped falling, an almighty rumble of thunder sent a HUGE crack slicing through the forest floor.

Ray, Droplett and Snowden held on to a nearby tree for dear life, waiting for the growling to calm down, hoping the ground would stop splitting!

'The Rogues are EVERYWHERE,' said Ray, breathing quickly. 'And it's only going to get worse. We have to hurry!'

'But where do we go?!' cried Droplett. 'We don't know where the Sky Crystal is!'

Hail-geese began to fall again.

'Maybe we should go back to the Weatherlands before we get GOOSED to death?!' yelled Coo La La. 'This is NOT how I saw myself dying!'

'I can't bind Tornadia's magic without BOTH of the Forever Crystals . . .' Ray replied.

'But the Sky Crystal could be anywhere,' said Coo La La.

'I would say it's here on Earth *somewhere*, since the Earth Crystal and the staff were both on Earth too,' said Snowden. 'Maybe the Sky Crystal got swept up in Tornadia's one-hundred-year storm after the Rainbow Weatherlings had their magic taken away.'

'Well, that narrows it down,' said Coo La La sarcastically. 'TO THE WHOLE WORLD.'

Ray knew he was right. She tried so hard to stay positive but it was REALLY hard when the whole world was counting on you, geese were falling from the skies, and the one thing you needed to stop the worst Rogue in history was proving very hard to find.

Ray thought desperately about what to try next. Snowflakes poured from Snowden's ears as he struggled to think of a plan, while Droplett became more agitated by the second.

'If I had my rain cape I'd be able to puddle-port us out of here! I have zero control of my magic without it. ARRRGH!' She threw her arms up in the air accidentally firing out jets of water from both hands. Droplett brought her arms down quickly.

Ray felt as frustrated as Droplett. 'I just wish there was an easier way to find the Sky Crystal!' she said, twiddling her blue streak of hair. 'I'm full of these gifts and yet I can't think of anything . . .' Then she gasped loudly.

'Is that a *good* gasp or a bad gasp?!' asked Snowden.

Ray began to smile and Nim meowed joyfully. 'I'm hoping it's a good one,' she said, eyes wide as an idea unfurled in her head. 'RETRIEVE!' she bellowed.

'Um . . . what?' said Coo La La.

Snowden's eyes widened. 'YES!'

'I can use Rainbow Retrieve's gift to find lost weather and stuff . . .' said Ray, spinning her staff around and accidentally sending it flying into a nearby tree. 'If the Sky Crystal is made of *pure weather*, then surely using Rainbow Retrieve's gift would find it?'

'You could be on to something, Ray,' said Snowden. 'AND you've practised this gift before!'

'Even if you DID end up retrieving an unwanted fog goblin,' Droplett added with a wink.

Ray picked up her staff with its new Earth Crystal glimmering in the darkness. The wind was howling, tearing through the forest, but Ray was determined to make this work.

'Guys, can you hold on to my shoulders so I don't get swept away?' she asked. Her friends were there in a second, hands firmly placed on both of Ray's shoulders, steadying her as she wrapped both hands around her staff. Ray remembered the time she'd practised this particular gift with La Blaze in the Rainburrow.

'Firstly, one must focus on WHAT needs to be found,' La Blaze had told her.

Lightning struck just a few metres away from Coo La La.

'If you can perform this gift quicker, that would be much appreciated,' he squeaked.

Ray thought about the Sky Crystal and how she NEEDED to find it.

'Once your focus is entirely on the lost thing, you point your staff upwards,' said La Blaze's voice. Ray kept her mind fixed on the Sky Crystal, concentrating hard even though she felt as if she might get blown away any minute now. She felt her magic fill up inside her, pouring through her fingertips and through the staff. A long,

155

wispy rainbow zoomed through the air, but then it disappeared as fast as it had been summoned.

'That's strange,' muttered Ray. 'Let me try again.'

But just like before, the wispy rainbow simply faded away.

'Maybe it's too windy?' suggested Droplett.

'Or maybe the Sky Crystal is too far away?' Snowden added, biting his lip. 'Is there a limit to how far this gift of retrieving weather can go?' he asked.

'When I learned about it, the notes said there were no limits,' said Ray. 'But maybe my magic just isn't strong enough yet? I haven't even had it for a year . . .

'Well, BE stronger,' said Coo La La simply. The friends stared at the pigeon in disbelief.

'Y'know, I can just break the rules again and splosh him without my cape,' said Droplett as another rumble of thunder sent the friends stumbling sideways.

But Ray managed to stay on two feet and clenched a fist. 'Coo La La is right. I HAVE to be stronger . . .'

CHAPTER 15

THE RAINBOW TRAIL

There was a strange sizzling noise above before fizzy rain began to pour down upon the friends.

'This is NOT helping!' Coo La La screamed up at the treetops.

But the rain got heavier and fizzier.

Coo La La adjusted his monocle and clenched his wings. 'I've had enough of these absolute stinkers!' He flew upwards against the rain, disappearing through the tops of the trees.

There was a squeal from above, a SLAP, a CLAP and a 'That'll serve you right, you big toenail!' and the rain began to calm down.

Ray didn't waste any time. She focused on the task in hand once again. She thought about the Sky Crystal – NOTHING BUT THE SKY CRYSTAL – and pointed her staff upwards. The rainbow weather magic filled up inside her, and a long, ethereal wisp of colour burst from the top of her staff.

'It's working!' she cried. But then the rainbow trail turned back on itself and disappeared. Ray slumped to the ground, staring at the staff. The Earth Crystal made from pure Glimmer was shining brightly in the darkness, creating a warm green glow on her skin, and suddenly it was as if a green light had also been ignited in her brain.

'The Glimmer!' said Ray, almost unable to get the words out fast enough. 'The Earth Crystal is made of Glimmer, and that helps to enhance my gifts, but we need MORE! Mother Root said that when trees are happy, they produce Glimmer. So, if we make the trees feel REALLY happy, maybe they'll produce enough Glimmer to help strengthen my magic?'

'That's a GREAT idea!' said a familiar voice, making the friends jump.

'Twiglett!' cried Ray happily as the tiny Woodling ran in for a hug.

'We can help you make the trees happier!'

Twiglett chimed in.

'And how do you suggest we cheer up a tree?' asked Coo La La, raising an eyebrow.

'What makes YOU feel happy?' said Twiglett.

'Lasagne?' said Coo La La. 'Or maybe that's just me . . .'

Nim mewed and wrapped himself around Ray's shoulders. She breathed in his floofy cloud scent and felt his warmth surround her. 'I love hugs,' she said softly.

'And so do the trees,' said Twiglett.

'Wait . . . so you're saying we HUG the trees?' asked Droplett, looking bemused.

'Exactly!' sang Twiglett, skipping over to a tree sapling and giving it a big cuddle. Tiny, glittery green specks began to rise up from the plant.

'Ray pointed to a huge tree a few metres away. 'I bet that one could produce a lot of Glimmer!' She ran up to the tree and wrapped her arms around it, hugging the trunk tight and letting her love for nature pour from her heart. Tiny twinkles of green glow engulfed Ray as if hugging her back.

'GROUP HUG!' cheered Droplett running to Ray's tree and spreading her arms out.

Coo La La joined the friends and took in a deep breath. 'I've never felt so calm,' he said, closing his eyes.

Snowden completed the big tree hug as the friends held on to each other's hands.

One by one, more Woodlings emerged, adding to the mighty hug, and soon green sparkles filled the air, flowing from the tree's roots, up through its bark and branches.

Ray closed her eyes and let the Glimmer surround her. She felt STRONGER. Just like she'd felt when she touched the Earth Crystal. She took a deep breath and opened her eyes again. Her skin looked as if it was made of shimmery green velvet!

'You're positively sparkling!' cheered Coo La La.

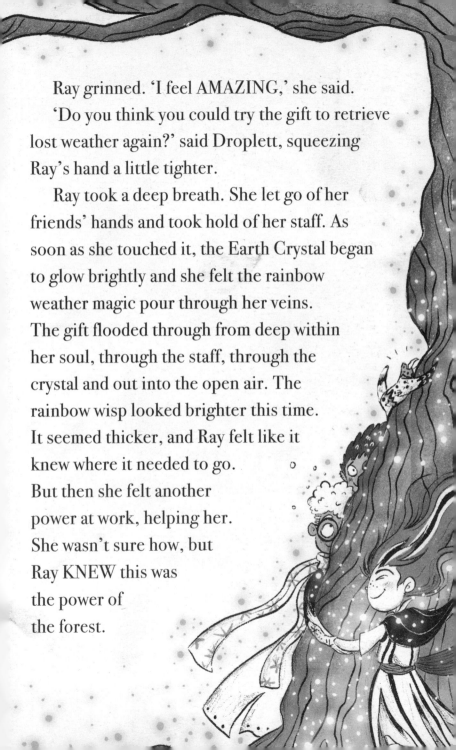

Ray grinned. 'I feel AMAZING,' she said.

'Do you think you could try the gift to retrieve lost weather again?' said Droplett, squeezing Ray's hand a little tighter.

Ray took a deep breath. She let go of her friends' hands and took hold of her staff. As soon as she touched it, the Earth Crystal began to glow brightly and she felt the rainbow weather magic pour through her veins. The gift flooded through from deep within her soul, through the staff, through the crystal and out into the open air. The rainbow wisp looked brighter this time. It seemed thicker, and Ray felt like it knew where it needed to go. But then she felt another power at work, helping her. She wasn't sure how, but Ray KNEW this was the power of the forest.

Ray concentrated even harder, thinking ONLY about the fact she needed to find the Sky Crystal. Ray's magic flowed through the tree roots, creating a beautiful glow of tangled pathways. Then her skin stopped sparkling and the Earth Crystal in her staff stopped glowing. The glowing roots dimmed.

The friends were silent.

'Well, that was an anticlimax,' said Coo La La.

Snowden's ears popped with snowflakes. 'I was sure it would work this time. I don't understand . . .' he muttered.

But Ray was smiling. 'Oh, but it DID work,' she said, pointing down at her feet. 'Look!'

165

CHAPTER 16
78 NETTLE DRIVE ENGLAND

A long, wiggly rainbow path began stretching out in front of Ray. It shone like a beacon of hope in the darkness. The path began snaking all the way through the trees into the distance. Snowden, Droplett and Coo La La clambered over and stared at where the beginning of the rainbow path sparkled at Ray's feet.

'Does that mean the gift worked?' asked Droplett hopefully.

'I think it does,' said Ray, laughing with relief.

Snowden's left ear was positively pouring with snowflakes. 'Glimmer is AMAZING,' he said, to nobody in particular.

Ray wriggled around in excitement. 'CELEBRATORY HIGH FIVE!' she cheered, and everyone completely missed.

'We'll try that again later,' Snowden winked.

'Let's follow the rainbow road!' Ray sang (rather badly).

Nim spun in the air before expanding to the size of a double bed. Ray swung herself on to his cloudy back followed by Droplett, Snowden and Coo La La at the rear.

As Ray and her friends took to the stormy skies, lightning flashes illuminated the darkness, and spiky, icy snowflakes zipped through the air. Luckily Nim expanded his chest, shielding them from the impact – a large, cloudy six-pack forming as the cloud-cat grew in size. The glowing red eyes of evil cloud-creatures lurked in the shadows as the bright rainbow trail before them stretched for miles and miles, beyond the forest and over vast oceans.

Absolutely nothing about the Earth's climate felt right. Blizzards raged in deserts that had never seen snow before. Snowmen marched across the equator and cities were fast becoming lagoons as the rain fell like an ocean from the sky.

168

The rainbow trail led the friends to a small island. As they approached, Ray felt a warmth hit her face. There was something strange about it. As they flew further, guided by the wispy colours, the temperature became hotter and hotter. Sweat dribbled down Ray's cheeks and water poured from Snowden's ears instead of snowflakes.

'Where are we?' said Ray.

Coo La La sniffed the air and lifted a wing. 'I know this place,' he said, closing his eyes in deep concentration. 'The sounds of kettles boiling in a crisis, the dunking of biscuits in tea . . . the scent of fish and chips . . . and suddenly I have an overwhelming need to queue somewhere . . . Why, of course, we're in England!'

'This is WAY too hot for England,' shrieked Droplett. 'Even I know that!'

'The Rogues are messing with their thermometers,' said Ray, feeling her hair stick to her wet forehead. 'Right now, there are no rules. While Tornadia is destroying the Weatherlands, and the Council of Forecasters are trapped in her awful snot-nado, they can't monitor the Earth's weather activity.'

The rainbow trail led Nim and the friends through cobbled streets and higgledy-piggledy towns, to tiny villages and beyond.

Ray found herself so distracted by what she could have sworn was a large chalk person etched into the side of a hill during a very bright flash of lightning, that she didn't see the rainbow trail coming to an end at a small cottage in the middle of the countryside. She also didn't see the young boy standing silhouetted at the open window, staring up in disbelief at the friends and a pigeon in a monocle riding upon a muscly cloud-cat.

Nim picked up speed, purring deeply and flying faster, following the trail with determination.

The rainbow path coursed all the way down, straight through the window and past the boy at 78 Nettle Drive, England.

'NIM!' cried Ray. 'STOOOOOP!'

But it was too late. Nim exploded. The friends went crashing into a large shelf full of action figures. Ray got to her feet in a panic. 'I think we just flew into someone's HOUSE!' she squeaked. 'A human house!'

'And there are tiny plastic people all over the floor!' shrieked Coo La La.

'Hello?' came a shy voice.

Ray, Snowden and Droplett froze on the spot. Nim reappeared as a head and tail, and Coo La La kicked at one of the toy figures.

A boy with large eyes and even larger hair was standing next to the window, dimly lit by large candles sitting on the ledge. He looked about the same age as Ray and he was wearing a black T-shirt with a green alien on its front. He crouched down slowly, not taking his eyes off the friends, before picking up Ray's staff.

'Um, I think you might have dropped this?' he said, stepping forward cautiously and handing it over. Ray was relieved to see that the Earth Crystal was still intact.

171

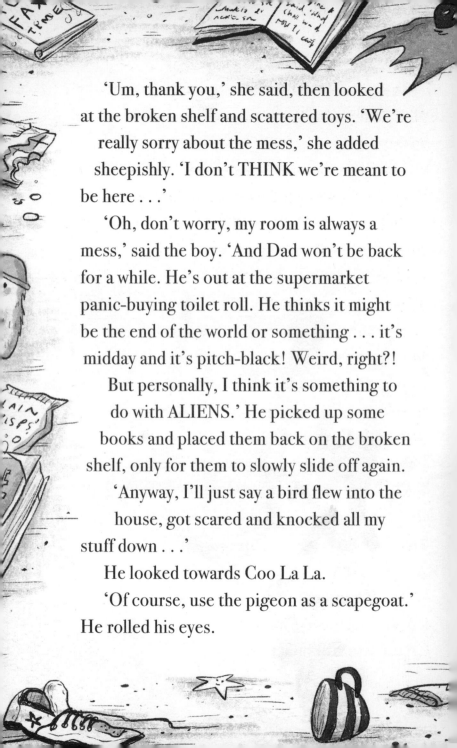

'Um, thank you,' she said, then looked at the broken shelf and scattered toys. 'We're really sorry about the mess,' she added sheepishly. 'I don't THINK we're meant to be here . . .'

'Oh, don't worry, my room is always a mess,' said the boy. 'And Dad won't be back for a while. He's out at the supermarket panic-buying toilet roll. He thinks it might be the end of the world or something . . . it's midday and it's pitch-black! Weird, right?!

But personally, I think it's something to do with ALIENS.' He picked up some books and placed them back on the broken shelf, only for them to slowly slide off again.

'Anyway, I'll just say a bird flew into the house, got scared and knocked all my stuff down . . .'

He looked towards Coo La La.

'Of course, use the pigeon as a scapegoat.' He rolled his eyes.

A two-headed
Nim floated slowly over
to the boy.

'Is that some *rare breed* of cat?
And is it . . . all right?' squeaked the boy.

'Don't worry!' Ray added quickly,
retrieving the rather misshapen cloud-
creature. 'He does that all the time.
This is my cloud-cat, Nim.'

The boy looked surprised. Ray
feared his eyes might roll out of his head
any second now. He pointed towards the
long, wispy rainbow flowing through his
bedroom window. 'Did you make
all those colours? Who ARE you guys?'
he asked in a high-pitched voice.

'If we tell you, we may have to
kill you,' said Coo La La a little
too seriously.

'Come on, guys, MAYBE the
rainbow trail led us here for a

reason and *maybe* the human can help us,' said Ray. 'What do we have to lose?'

'Oh, not much . . . only the WHOLE WORLD,' Coo La La answered flatly.

Ignoring the pigeon, Ray turned back to the boy. 'I'm Ray Grey . . . and these are my best friends Snowden Everfreeze and Droplett Dewbells.'

Coo La La cleared his throat loudly.

'And that's Coo La La,' added Ray. 'You're probably wondering why we're here, and well, as you can see, my rainbow trail led us here. The truth is, we're meant to be finding something VERY important.'

'Well, er, I'm Klaus Bottomly,' said the boy. 'And there was a lot of information in your introduction that I'm not entirely sure I understand.' He paused and looked a

174

little awkward. 'Are you *aliens*? Did you make the world go dark?'

'I'm not sure we need to answer that,' said Coo La La quickly.

'In a way; we do have something to do with it,' said Ray giving the pigeon a please-be-quiet kind of glance. 'But the main thing is . . . we're here to make it right.'

CHAPTER 17
FINDING THE IMPORTANT THING

'So, I was right?' said Klaus, looking excited. 'You're *aliens*?!'

'We're not *aliens* . . .' said Snowden. 'We're *Weatherlings* . . .'

'And I'm a *pigeon*,' added Coo La La.

Klaus blinked a few times. 'Is it possible I'm more confused than before?'

'We don't have time to explain,' said Ray quickly. 'But Weatherlings create the weather on Earth . . .'

'And some of them make bad weather,' added Snowden.

'And ONE of those baddies destroyed the big Sunflower in the sky,' said Droplett. 'Known to *you* as the sun.'

'And we really, really need to stop a VERY bad

177

lady from completely ruining our home in the sky and turning Earth into a STORM PLANET. But I have to find the really important thing before I can do anything . . .' finished Ray.

'And I should add that I *was* having a perfectly nice bath until all this kicked off,' Coo La La chipped in.

Klaus was very quiet. 'OK . . .' he finally said.

'You didn't understand a word of what we just said, did you?' said Coo La La.

'Nope,' said Klaus. 'But I understand that YOU are a pigeon and you like baths.'

'Well, I'm a bit *more* than that,' said Coo La La, looking offended. 'I also like lasagne.'

'So, let me try to make sense of this . . . A magical rainbow trail led you here? To THIS house? Seventy-eight Nettle Drive?' asked Klaus, rubbing his forehead.

Ray nodded, noticing that the wispy rainbow path wiggled around the room all the way into a tall glass cabinet at the far corner. The colourful light illuminated the objects inside.

Ray made her way over to the cabinet, trying not to step on a cuddly yeti toy and comics about evil penguins taking over the world.

'I'm not sure that you're going to find anything world-savingly important in my rock collection,' said Klaus with a chuckle.

But Ray noticed the rainbow engulfed one round, dark object. She pressed her face against the glass and felt a rush of magic surge through her. Where the rainbow trail had ended, the dark object began to glow a bright blue.

'Wow! It never usually glows by itself!' Klaus gasped.

'This is it,' whispered Ray. 'This is the Sky Crystal!'

The Earth Crystal in Ray's staff began to glow too. The bright green and blue of the Forever Crystals illuminated the walls of the bedroom.

'Why does Klaus Bottomly of seventy-eight Nettle Drive have the Sky Crystal?!' spluttered Coo La La.

'That's a family heirloom,' said Klaus.

Ray took a deep breath.

179

'I know this may seem very strange at the moment, and a bit unreal,' she said gently. 'But that family heirloom of yours is the one thing that can save the world. We really need it.'

Klaus raised an eyebrow. 'Well, if that's the case . . . it's yours.' He opened the cabinet before grabbing the blue crystal. It started to glow a little brighter. 'Cool, isn't it,' he said with a smile. 'It always glows a little bit when I hold it. It never glows quite as much as it does with you, though!' He offered the crystal to Ray. 'I'll be sad to say goodbye, but if you need it to save the world, then it's yours. It's what my mum would've wanted too.'

'Thank you,' said Ray taking the Sky Crystal. She immediately felt its power surge through her body. Even her hair appeared to glow a little brighter!

'Well, Klaus Bottomly, you may have just helped to stop a TERRIBLE Rogue and save everything,' said Ray with a big grin. 'Pretty cool, huh?'

'I didn't think it could get any cooler than speaking to MAGICAL beings who live in the sky, AND a pigeon!' he said breathlessly. He turned to Coo La La with wide eyes. 'Can ALL pigeons talk?'

'Of course they can,' said Coo La La as if it was the most obvious thing in the world. 'But only Weatherlings can hear us.'

181

Everyone was quiet for a moment.

'Actually, that can't be right . . .' said Coo La La with a nervous laugh. 'This boy is a HUMAN and he can hear me.'

They paused for another moment and then, as Ray looked back at Klaus, she swore in the dim candlelight that one of his eyes glimmered purple and the other blue . . . but an almighty CRACKLE of lightning and a roar of thunder made the friends jump. 'We have to go!' said Ray, gripping the Sky Crystal. 'Sorry to have to shoot off. We're running out of time!'

Nim stretched out for the friends to sit on.

'Good luck saving the world,' said Klaus with a small wave as Ray leaped on to the cloud-cat's back, her staff in one hand and the reclaimed Sky Crystal in the other. 'I hope to meet you again some day!'

CHAPTER 18

THE CAVERN OF THE BOUND

As Nim flew higher and higher towards the Weatherlands, Ray's mind was positively swirling. She took a few deep, calming breaths. She now had everything she needed to bind Tornadia's magic. But she still didn't know HOW to do it! Ray placed the bright blue Sky Crystal in the empty circle of her staff and immediately everything went blurry. She lost sight of everything around her as rainbow weather magic flooded through her. She blinked a few times.

As her eyes adjusted, Ray realised that she was somewhere completely different, standing in a huge grotto. Surrounding the rocky walls were tiny, round objects arranged neatly along rocky shelves that stretched upwards as far as the eye could see. Ray walked over to the lowest shelf. The objects upon it looked like shimmery glass globes, roughly the size of Ray's palm. On closer inspection, Ray could see something moving around inside each of the globes, and there was a small plaque in front of each one.

'*Eddie Blizzard*,' Ray read aloud. She frowned. 'I remember studying this Rogue in class once – Eddie created one of the worst snowstorms in history.' She looked at the small globe sitting behind the name plaque. Tiny snowflakes were gently falling; an infinite flurry of sparkly white specks.

Ray moved along to the next plaque.

'*Kalamity Killbreeze*.' She gasped. 'Wait . . . Kalamity was responsible for the terrible hurricane that blew everyone's houses from Canada into the Arctic Ocean!'

Ray continued to read the next few plaques. '*Galveston Gustworthy* . . . I'm pretty sure he was the creator of the Great Storm of 1900. He was TERRIBLE.'

186

The next plaque read: *Ebafreezer Scrooge*. Ray growled. 'I've heard all about YOU . . . creating hailstones the size of ducks in northern India. How could you?!'

The last name plaque said: *Tornadia Twist* but it had no globe behind it. Just an empty space. As Ray looked around her, her staff pulsating with blue and green light from the Forever Crystals, she realised that the globes contained weather magic . . . weather magic that had once belonged to some of the worst Rogues in history. She found herself saying out loud: 'The CAVERN OF THE BOUND . . .'

'THIS is where a Rogue's magic goes once it's bound!' Ray looked at her staff. 'But how do I know this will work?' she said to herself. 'I can't exactly practise this gift on anyone.'

Shimmering lights appeared in the centre of the grotto. The lights danced and rearranged themselves, as if made from silky water before creating a beautiful rainbow.

Ray found herself transfixed as the colours

made whispering sounds. Were the colours speaking? But then she remembered something Coo La La had said in the classroom of the underground Rainbow Academy.

'*Don't just SEE the colours. Feel them . . . And most importantly HEAR them,*' Ray recited.

She had always *felt* her rainbow weather magic pouring through her – it was warm and tingly and that nice feeling you get when you're excited about something. And sure, Ray had always *seen* her rainbow weather magic. But she'd hadn't yet HEARD it. Until now . . .

You must embrace all types of weather
Only then can the crystals work together,
Trust in your gift, the colours
will guide you . . .
You'll know just what you need to do.

Ray stared at the empty space behind Tornadia's name plaque and gripped her staff tightly.

Everything went blurry. There was a distant meow. Ray blinked and found herself back on Nim's floofy body, soaring through the air as if nothing had happened.

'Are you OK, Ray?' asked Snowden. 'You seemed really distracted for a moment.'

'Well, of course she's distracted,' said Coo La La. 'She's about to face TORNADIA TWIST!'

'Guys,' Ray said quickly. 'I know how to use my gift!'

'Wait, WHAT?' said Coo La La. '*How*?'

Ray lifted her staff and tapped the Forever Crystals lightly. 'Soooo, just a second ago, I kind of travelled to a place called the Cavern of the Bound . . .'

'Um, again . . . WHAT?' repeated Coo La La.

'But you've been here, flying with us the whole time,' said Droplett, looking concerned.

'I don't actually know how I got there. Or how I got back here again after . . . I think part of me . . . the magical, rainbow part of me, was in the Cavern of the Bound.'

'That sounds both cool and creepy,' said Coo La La, shuffling back a little.

A single snowflake popped out of both Snowden's ears at the same time. 'What is this Cavern of the Bound exactly?' he asked.

'It's where all the worst Rogues' magic is kept. All the previous Rainbow Weatherlings with the gift to bind must have put them there,' said Ray. 'There's an empty spot ready for Tornadia, and I'm going to make sure that it's filled with her evil rainbow magic.'

TORNADIA TWIST

CHAPTER 19

STORM CITY

The Weatherlands, or what was left of them, shimmered into view. Every pod house in the Cloudimulus Suburbs was gone, the Valley of Winds was in cloudy pieces and the Flurry Mountains were scorched and charred as lightning-nados sizzled around them. The umbrellas of Dripping-Down Village were scattered amongst the Crackling Caves next door, which was now mostly rubble – explosions of lightning sending the fragments into space, while Tornadia and her team of Rogues slowly turned the Earth and skies into their stormy playground.

Ray's heart ached for her home. The school for SunKeepers was gone. Sky Academy was gone. The Council of Forecasters headquarters was gone. Only parts of the Forest of Fahrenheits remained.

Evil cloud-creatures filled the dark skies ahead, barely visible apart from their red glowing eyes that illuminated their grey cloudy bodies. Ray watched in horror as she recognised her dad's cloud-creature Waldo float past in some kind of hypnotised state. He didn't look anything like the Waldo she knew . . . His eyes were lifeless and red, and his body a murky grey. He lolloped along with the other zombie-like cloud-creatures.

'They're all flocking the same way . . .' said Snowden, pointing to the mass of grey clouds heading in the direction of the Forest of Fahrenheits.

'Tornadia must be summoning them. If we follow the evil cloud-creatures, we might find her . . .' Ray gulped. 'Then I can bind her magic once and for all.'

Nim surged forward after them. He followed the hoard of hypnotised clouds and Ray could hear panicked Cloud Weatherlings calling out desperately for their cloud-companions.

'Victor!'

194

'Hugo!'
'Where's Chloeeee?!'
'Pedroooo!'
'Douglasssss!
'Kirk! My previous Kirk!'

Ray's heart felt heavy. She knew that while their cloud-companions were in Tornadia's control, there was nothing they could do to stop her.

'WAAAALDO!' cried a familiar voice. The same voice then shouted, 'RAAAAAAY! WHERE ARE YOUUU?!'

'Dad?!' Ray croaked, pointing her illuminated staff towards the trees below. All she wanted to do was fly down and give him a big hug. Her dad's hugs always made her feel better. But right now, she had to find Tornadia.

Ray could hear the shouts of terrified Weatherlings running through the forest below. They were heading in the same direction that Ray was flying: after the hypnotised cloud-creatures. Then she remembered something

195

that made her blood run cold.

'Mr Current told us that everyone was gathering at the Weatherstone Circle,' Ray said. 'If Tornadia is there too, then she'll have EVERYONE'S magic in her control!'

She leaned back suddenly and Nim skidded to a halt in the air with a jolt. Coo La La almost rolled off backwards, grabbing on to Snowden's scarf just in time.

'You're a PIGEON. You CAN fly, you know!' Snowden choked as Coo La La scaled back up his scarf.

A little way beyond, a small patch of the forest was illuminated as sparks of purple lightning fired through the air and knicker-nados swirled violently. The red-eyed cloud-creatures circled the area. Ray flinched as a menacing laugh echoed across the skies followed by a great roar of thunder.

'I *think* we may have found Tornadia . . .' muttered Snowden.

'I think SHE'S found every single pair of

knickers in the Weatherlands,' added Droplett.

A thick fog began to roll in.

'We need to land, so we can get as close to Tornadia as possible before we lose our way in the fog,' said Ray. Nim lowered the friends gently to the forest floor. Ray rubbed him behind the ears affectionately before sliding off of his back. 'You're brilliant, Nim,' she whispered into his floofy body. 'I love you.'

Ray dimmed her staff a little as the friends tiptoed their way through the dark, foggy forest.

Ray was careful to avoid the puff pod patch, where the baby clouds were still growing. But as the low light of her staff shone upon the spotty round plants, she noticed that they were wilting. Of course . . . without sunlight they would die!

Ray picked up the pace. Every minute the big Sunflower in the sky wasn't shining, was another minute closer to the end of the Weatherlands and the Earth as they knew it.

With the darkness and the thick fog, it was near impossible to see anything, even with Ray's staff illuminated. But despite not being able to see, Ray knew this patch of the forest well. She carried on marching towards the sounds of evil laughter and shocked gasps.

'Wait!' said Snowden, grabbing her hand. 'We need to make you less noticeable,' he held a gloved hand to the air. 'I think it's time for my custom snow-wig trick.'

Using his snow magic, Snowden drew an intricate snowflake in the air. After making his final marks, it hovered for a moment then began to weave through the air, dancing around Ray's head. Ray lifted her hair up so that the whole lot was tucked safely inside the rather fetching snow-white beehive on her head.

'Thanks, Snowden, you're amazing,' she said, patting the pile of cold snow. Ray extinguished her rainbow staff, following Tornadia's evil laughs and the purple flashes of light to guide their way. She felt a cold sense of dread running through her veins (unless that was just cold of the snow wig . . .) and almost bumped into a wall of Weatherlings blocking the rest of the way.

'Stay back, children!' said a kindly old Weatherling shaking with fear. 'It's not safe here!'

But Ray carried on pushing her way through the crowd.

'Ray?! Is that YOU?' said two familiar voices.

Ray could make out Frazzle and Fump's faces next to her. She put a finger to her mouth. 'Shhhh. I can't let Tornadia know I'm here yet . . .' she whispered. 'I'm going to try to bind her magic while she's not looking.'

'Wait? WHAT? How will you –' Fump began, but Frazzle slapped a hand over his mouth urging him to be quiet. Fump mouthed the word SORRY before both of the Striker twins stood up straight and saluted.

They placed themselves in front of Ray to keep her hidden, then Frazzle leaned in and said as quietly as possible, 'Tornadia's right over there . . .' She took Ray's hand gently.

The twins stayed in front of Ray as she moved through the horde of Weatherlings. Finally, the centre of the stone circle came into view, floodlit by the bright purple sparks crackling around the tall, stripy-haired woman.

There was absolutely no doubt it was Tornadia Twist. She was standing by the Rainbow Weatherstone, and next to her were . . . Snowden and Droplett!

Ray turned to find her friends were no longer behind her. She almost shouted out, but she clamped her hands around her mouth just in time. Ray couldn't give herself away now. This was her chance. She needed to use her binding gift NOW.

Ray gripped her staff tightly and closed her eyes. The air shifted. But a shiver ran down her spine as she was overcome by a strange feeling. The kind of feeling you get when you realise there's somebody else with you in an otherwise empty room.

'FINALLY!' Tornadia's voice sang.

Ray opened her eyes to find Tornadia standing centimetres away from her. Ray's heart dropped as a huge grin spread over the Rainbow Rogue's face. 'I've been waiting for you, darling.'

CHAPTER 20

FACE TO FACE

'Tornadia, please let my friends go,' Ray said in a shaky voice.

Tornadia raised her eyebrows. 'Since you asked so politely.'

With one click of her fingers she sent Snowden and Droplett disappearing into a swirling puddle. Nim hissed and flew full speed towards the terrifying whirlpool with a satisfying plop.

'NOOOOOOOOOOO!' shrieked Ray, lurching towards Tornadia, staff outstretched. But a burst of hot air sent her flying backwards through the crowd.

Frazzle and Fump rushed to help Ray to her feet. But the twins were dragged through the air feet first by a black and white striped rainbow. The monotone band threw them into the violent, swirling puddle trap, then within the blink of an eye, the whirlpool was gone.

Fury swooshed through Ray.

'TORNADIA!' she roared. 'WHERE HAVE YOU SENT THEM?!' She pointed her staff towards the Rogue, breathing deeply. 'This is between US, so back off and leave my friends alone!'

But Tornadia burst out laughing.

'Darling, I must THANK you,' she said, tilting her head to one side ominously. 'That little plopping me into the puddle trick you did the last time we met was my inspiration.'

Ray swallowed hard.

'What a brilliant way to get Weatherlings out of the way!' Tornadia trilled. She looked around at the crowd and giggled hysterically. 'That's right, RAINBOW GREY inspired *me*. You can thank her for all *this*!'

Tornadia threw her arms up and rose into the air, elevated by a spindly tornado wrapped around the bottom half of her body like a vicious mermaid tail. As she rose higher and higher, the Rogue

conjured at least fifteen HUGE snow monsters
using the snow magic of every Snow Weatherling
around her. Ray noticed the Snow Weatherlings
wincing, their knees buckling,
as if Tornadia's control of their power was slowly
weakening them.

Each of the snow monsters stepped forward
menacingly, their eyes flashing a bright
glowing red.

'Why do *all of* Tornadia's evil creations have
red eyes? She has NO creativity,' piped up Coo
La La, who'd spent the past five minutes circling
above Tornadia trying to aim a poo at her head.

The Rogue swung her arms forward, sending
a huge gust of wind around the crowd. Trees
began to fall sideways, each trunk tumbling to
the forest floor with an almighty thud.

Even though she couldn't see it, Ray could
sense the shadowy tendrils rising up from the
broken trunks. She could already feel its presence
dampening her magic. Tornadia laughed as the
Shadow Essence silently weaved its way through

the air in Ray's direction searching for something to feed on – *rainbow weather magic.*

But what Ray couldn't understand was why the Shadow Essence wasn't aiming for Tornadia's power too. Tornadia was a Rogue Rainbow Weatherling after all.

Seeing Ray's confused expression, Tornadia laughed even louder.

'Darling, the magic left inside me isn't what the Shadow Essence desires any more,' she sang. She let another black and white rainbow splurge from her palm; there was nothing good about that 'rainbow' at all.

'You're . . . you're too evil for the Shadow Essence,' Ray stammered, hardly able to believe what she was seeing. 'I didn't think that was even *possible* . . .'

'Darling, with me ANYTHING is possible!' cried Tornadia, letting her evil stripes flood the area, guiding the Shadow Essence along with it.

Ray felt the dense trails of essence and dark rainbow magic heading towards her. Dark magic, forbidden magic, had the ability to extinguish every ounce of hope and love left inside you. And Ray realised that this is exactly what had happened to Tornadia. She had no hope and no love left. Instead of anger, Ray felt a deep sense of sadness for the Rogue.

'RAY!' cried a familiar voice. She felt someone take her hand.

The Shadow Essence slithered around the tree roots, snaking towards Ray at super speed.

'But I need to save my friends!' Ray sobbed. Her eyes were blurry with tears.

'They *will* be OK,' said a man's voice breathlessly. 'Those kids are tougher than a batch of stale rumblebuns!'

Ray felt the Weatherling's arms wrap around her, lifting her up. 'The Shadow Essence will have to get through ME first! Nobody messes with my Ray-Ray!'

Ray wiped at her eyes. 'DAD?!' she spluttered.

She threw her arms around his neck,

breathing in the familiar musty scent. She felt his prickly beard on her cheek. She appreciated what he was trying to do, but Ray knew it wouldn't make any difference. They could keep on running, but the Shadow Essence would not stop following. It would eventually catch up. Ray couldn't forget how the Shadow Essence hadn't affected Tornadia any more. Years of forbidden magic and seeking revenge had darkened her soul beyond repair.

But surely there HAD to be something . . . the teeniest, tiniest glimmer of something GOOD inside Tornadia? Ray always saw the good in EVERYONE. Surely everybody had the potential to learn . . . to *grow*. Just like La Blaze had done.

The thought of La Blaze gave Ray a new burst of energy. She peered up at the skies. Between the smudges of evil clouds and prickly lightning, she spotted a bright star, shining brighter than the rest.

La Blaze was always there with her . . .

Everyone was with her. It was time.

Ray kissed her dad on the cheek and lifted her staff. She pulled the staff over her head as if to create a huge paint stroke.

'Ray?! What are you doing?!' Haze cried as a

rainbow poured from the end of the staff.
The Forever Crystals pulsed brightly. Ray had
never created a rainbow slide quite so big and
bright! She climbed up on to her dad's shoulder
and launched herself at the rainbow slide
stretched out in front of her.

'Wait! Ray-Ray!' Haze cried, trying to pull
Ray back to him.

But Ray was already surfing the colourful
bands back to the Weatherstone Circle. The
rainbow slide illuminated the forest below . . .
the only light in the darkness. She knew what
she had to do. She was Rainbow Grey and
she NEVER gave up!

CHAPTER 21
DEAL!

Ray saw Tornadia and her cyclone tail spinning violently above the stone circle.

The Rogue's laugh resounded across the skies. 'You just can't get enough, can you, Rainbow Grey?!' she mocked, throwing lightning bolts in Ray's direction.

Ray spun on the spot quickly, pressing her staff into the rainbow slide below. Using her gift from Rainbow Bubble, she created a protective forcefield around her, causing the lightning bolts to ricochet off the bubble shield, sizzling away to nothing. Ray couldn't help but feel pleased, she was using TWO gifts at once . . . she'd never done that before! She knew it must be the Forever Crystals working to help strengthen and control her rainbow weather magic.

Tornadia flew towards Ray, looking even more

determined than before. But for a split second Ray noticed a flicker of panic in the Rogue's eyes as she caught sight of Ray's staff, complete with the Earth Crystal and the Sky Crystal. She knew that Ray was ready to cast the most powerful gift of them all. The gift to bind another.

But Tornadia was oh-so powerful. She threw all of her strength into a HUGE rumble of thunder that shook the skies. It was so loud that Ray couldn't focus, and she felt her magic slip from her grip. The rainbow-bubble burst and the rainbow slide disappeared and before she knew it Ray was tumbling to the ground. The treetops approached at super speed and Tornadia's cackles echoed all around as she created vicious icicle spikes in the forest below. Ray braced herself for impact.

But then, with an almighty SWOOOOOOSH, Ray found herself on the back of a wind bugle. She was moving so fast, it was hard to catch her breath or realise WHO had saved her from becoming a pitter patter pin-cushion.

'Hold on tight!' yelled the familiar friendly voice of Gusty Gavin. The Sky Academy librarian raced through the trees at a speed Ray never thought any Wind Weatherling was capable of.

'How do you still have your magic?!' she shrieked, holding on to his waistcoat as tightly as she could. 'Tornadia has control of everyone around here!'

But then Ray noticed black-and-white streaks in Gavin's usual brown mop of hair. Just like Ray's. This was only a result of using banned magic from the *Book of Forbidden Forces*.

'It's a temporary enchantment on my wind instrument,' Gavin yelled back to Ray. 'Don't tell anyone!'

Ray couldn't quite believe it. Gavin was the one who had warned her never to use forbidden magic! 'I promise not to tell if YOU promise never to use forbidden magic ever again!' she replied through the screams of wind, roars of thunder and thrashing of icy hailstones.

'DEAL!' said Gavin as the wind bugle

began to wobble violently, throwing both
of the Weatherlings sideways.

Ray and Gusty Gavin went tumbling straight
into a large bluster bush. Ray was sure her bottom
must be one big bruise by now.

She coughed and spluttered as she felt around
for her staff. She opened her eyes and found
herself back inside the Weatherstone Circle.

'My staff?!' Ray croaked. 'Where's
my staff?!'

'HERE!' said a voice from above.
Percy was hidden among
the branches of one of
the only surviving
trees, looking
utterly terrified.
He retrieved Ray's
staff that had got
tangled up in some

nearby
branches
and threw it
towards her.

'Thanks, Percy!'
said Ray, catching the
staff and getting to her feet.
'Percy, you should get out of here, it's
not safe!'

'I know, but hugging something is one of
the only things that helps me calm down when
I'm feeling anxious.' He breathed in and out
slowly. 'Always has . . . but, well, I'M VERY
ANXIOUS right now, and so far, I've not been
swept away or plunged into a puddle or eaten
by snow monsters!'

This was bizarre since Tornadia had
destroyed most of the trees around him.
But then Ray spotted green sparkles dancing
around Percy's arms as he embraced the tree.

'The Glimmer is keeping you safe!' said Ray.

Screams and shouts grew in volume as Weatherlings scattered into the surrounding forest, attempting to get away from Tornadia. Others were desperately trying to use their magic against the Rogue. But it was no good. Tornadia had control of ALL the magic around her. Apart from Ray's.

Another huge tree collapsed to the floor as Tornadia tore through the forest into the Weatherstone Circle. There was something different about it. Then she realised that the only Weatherstone left standing was the Rainbow Stone. Every other stone had been destroyed, replaced by a pile of rubble. Ray felt sick. The Weatherlands' heritage – a sky-wide treasure – gone, just like that.

The dense, dark Shadow Essence slithered its way from the broken trees, heading straight for Ray.

'WHAT IS THAT?!' Percy squeaked, trying to waft the Shadow Essence away. He pressed himself into the tree trunk. Ray noticed something

218

odd as the Shadow Essence seemed to pass AROUND Percy before continuing towards her.

She could feel the effects of it straight away, weakening her.

'Why use up all that energy, darling?' said Tornadia, strolling through the Shadow Essence as if it were a harmless mist. 'You're just one kid,' she sneered. 'You can't make a difference.'

Just one kid . . .? Ray thought to herself . . . She stood up, leaning on her staff for support.

'You're right, Tornadia,' she croaked. 'I am just one kid. Snowden is just one kid, and so is Droplett . . . Frazzle is just one Weatherling, and so is Fump . . .'

'AND SO AM I!' yelled another voice. Within the murky mist, Ray spotted Percy with his hands on his hips.

'Oh, fog off,' said Tornadia, and with a waft of her left hand, sent Percy flying back into what was left of the Forest of Fahrenheits.

Ray looked into Tornadia's piercing blue and purple eyes.

'Each of us is "just one kid" but if EVERY "kid" tries to make a difference, then we become *lots* of kids making a difference. But the most important thing is that I have friends who stick by me, no matter what. And *together* we CAN make a difference!'

Tornadia blinked and yawned. 'Oh, sorry, darling, were you talking to me?' Two large icicles surged from her hands. 'I'm very bored now . . .'

She sent the icicles tearing through the mist. More trees exploded into pieces, releasing more Shadow Essence.

'Why don't you just *kill* me?' Ray said, barely able to get her words out.

Tornadia smirked. 'Who said anything about *ending* your life? I just need to end your magic, and I need you to be alive for the Shadow Essence to take it.' She folded her arms. 'It'll be over soon, darling. And once you're no threat to me any more, I couldn't care less what you do. You'll be NOTHING.'

The Shadow Essence was dense and thick and endless. Ray felt herself disappearing into its incessant darkness.

I can't give up, she thought to herself.

But she felt so weak.

'You'll be all right, Ray!' said a voice next to her. Percy emerged through the dark essence, covered in scratches. He grabbed Ray's arm but her knees buckled, and she fell to the ground.

'We can't let that windy fog-face take your magic, NO WAY!' cried Percy. 'How are you meant to get rid of this horrible shadowy stuff?!'

But Ray was too weak to reply. Percy hugged her tightly. Just like Snowden and Droplett and Frazzle and Fump (before they were all tossed into the puddle trap) he was sticking by her . . . no matter what. As she felt her eyes closing, Ray mustered up the TEENIEST, tiniest bit of strength to say, 'Trees . . . Hug . . . Glimmer . . .'

There was no answer. Ray noticed that Percy was no longer by her side. Everything was dark and silent.

CHAPTER 22

A HUG TO SAVE THE WORLD

Ray stirred. Her eyelids flickered open and she gradually felt her magic returning bit by bit as if her limbs were coming back to life after pins and needles.

She heard shouting. 'HUG THE TREEEEEES! IT'LL HELP RAAAAAY!'

Then something caught Ray's eye. Green sparkles among the darkness of the forest.

The sparkles were coming from one of the few trees still standing, and at the base of the trunk was Percy. He was hugging the tree with all his might. Gusty Gavin was embracing another.

Green sparkles poured out from the trunks as more and more Weatherlings got up from their hiding places and joined in. Like bright beacons of hope, one by one, the bright green glow of Glimmer was released from the happy trees. And as it spread through the air like twinkling fairy lights, it appeared to be dissolving the Shadow Essence.

Ray felt her magic slowly strengthening inside her. 'MORE Glimmer!' she croaked, a little louder this time, grinning as she saw Coo La La draped around the branch of a smaller tree, squeezing it with all his might.

'I LOVE YOU, TREE!' he sang at the top of his voice.

More and more Weatherlings followed suit, hugging any surviving tree they could.

Ray could feel the happiness erupting from the very soul of the Forest of Fahrenheits.

'What above Earth are you all DOING?!' shrieked Tornadia. She flung both arms outwards, sending hurricane-level winds towards her victims. But, weirdly, only a light breeze hit the Weatherlings in Tornadia's path.

'Well, that was rather nice,' Coo La La mocked. 'Feel free to do that again, Miss Twist.'

As Tornadia opened her mouth to respond, a large snowball flew into her face with a SPLAT.

Ray gasped as Snowden and Droplett soared through the shadowy mist on Nim's back.

'This is preposterous!' Tornadia screamed. 'I THREW YOU INTO A PUDDLE TRAP!' She hurled a black and white rainbow at Snowden, but it faded before it had a chance to reach him.

'Well, looks like we got out, doesn't it, you massive INCONVENIENCE!' yelled Droplett as the friends swooped down to the nearest tree and began hugging it.

Knowing that her best friends were safe, gave Ray a burst of strength.

She watched the sparkly Glimmer ooze from the surrounding tree trunks like glorious twinkles of life.

She breathed in deeply . . . embracing the pure love that she felt for all things. Her family. Her friends. Her home. The Earth. Everything.

227

Tornadia aimed her evil magic towards another large tree, but it was no good. Every tree still standing as far as the eye could see was being hugged by a Weatherling. And one by one, any magic once in Tornadia's grip slowly returned to its rightful owner.

'She's losing control!' thought Ray. 'HUG HARDER!' she called out.

Cloud-creatures swept down from the skies, their eyes no longer red. Waldo flew to Haze's side and rubbed his huge tail up against his companion before wrapping himself around a wibbly tree.

Tornadia looked both angry and completely confused.

'What is this?!' she spluttered. 'How does hugging a TREE make any of this happen?!'

'Because Glimmer represents all that is good, just like rainbow weather magic,' said Ray looking Tornadia straight in her blue and purple eyes. 'And good *always* wins.'

On the word 'WINS', Ray planted her staff

228

into the ground in front of her. Her rainbow gifts RAGED inside her. But there was only one gift she needed right now.

She closed her eyes tight remembering what she had heard in the Cavern of the Bound.

You must embrace all types of weather
Only then can the crystals work together,
Trust in your gift, the colours
will guide you ...
You'll know just what you need to do.

'I trust in my gift,' Ray said to herself. Tornadia's screams were merely whispers in the distance. All Ray could see were colours. All she could FEEL were colours. All she could HEAR were colours.

'*You must embrace all types of weather ...*' she repeated. 'I know just what I need to do ...'

She opened her eyes and pointed her staff in Snowden's direction. Immediately the brightest rainbow poured from the Forever Crystals,

229

taking hold of his magic.

'Just need to borrow some snow for a mo!' Ray called out with a wink. Snowden grinned and saluted, stepping forward and allowing Ray to embrace his power.

Droplett ran to Snowden's side. 'Have my rain!' she shouted.

Ray moved her staff around to Droplett, feeling the rain magic come to her. It made her fingertips tingle. Ray had never had control of more than one type of weather magic before; she wondered if she would be strong enough to take control of even MORE magic?

'Over here!' cried Gusty Gavin, running to join Droplett and Snowden. 'Take my wind!' he bellowed.

Ray guided her staff to where Gavin had his arms outstretched. She suddenly felt the rush of his wind magic breeze through her.

Snow, rain, wind . . .

Waldo flew to Ray's side. She saw her dad waving his cloud crook frantically before her. 'You've GOT this, Ray-Ray!'

She moved her staff around, gripping on to her dad's cloud magic, feeling the connection with Waldo as the cloud-creature hovered above her.

Then Frazzle and Fump stepped up and grinned at Ray.

'You can do it! What's ours is YOURS!'

KABOOM, KAZIIIING! The thunder and lightning magic felt *electrifying*!

231

Ray just needed one more type of weather magic. Sun magic. The most powerful of them all (aside from rainbow weather magic, of course!). Ray's heart ached. If only La Blaze were here, Ray knew she would have offered her magic in a heartbeat.

Ray took a deep breath. 'I need sun magic!' she called. But then she remembered that Tornadia had trapped all the SunKeepers in a bogie-nado . . .

'Seems your stupid little stunt isn't quite going to plan, is it?!' screamed Tornadia, charging towards Ray.

Tornadia reached out to Ray, so close they were almost touching, when an almighty flash of bright yellow sent the Rogue flying backwards. Five SunKeepers emerged from the light, their lemon hair flowing in the air like feathery wisps. Even though they were covered in bogies, they still looked mesmerising.

'Nobody destroys our Sunflower and gets away with it,' said one of the SunKeepers. Using her power, she zoomed forward towards Ray on a chair with huge sunflower wheels. She joined the line of Weatherlings sharing their magic and nodded at Ray. 'You can do this, Rainbow Grey!' she shouted.

Ray pointed her staff towards the Sun Weatherling and let the warmth of the sun magic pour into her soul.

This was it.

For the first time ever Ray had control of every type of weather magic.

CHAPTER 23
ALL THE MAGIC . . .

The Forever Crystals began to glow brighter and brighter in Ray's staff as the Glimmer protected her from the Shadow Essence and Tornadia's Rogue magic.

Ray had to stay focused. It wasn't easy holding on to so much power all at once . . . especially with so many gifts raging around inside her. And everything was enhanced by the Glimmer.

This was Ray's only chance. But Tornadia was resisting, her black and white rainbow thrashing against Ray's colours. Ray could feel the dark magic invading her own good magic.

Just one more push, she thought. Tornadia's evil rainbow forced its way forward bit by bit. Ray really had underestimated how STRONG the Rogue was. She wondered how much longer she could hold on to everyone's weather magic. Her vision began to wobble.

But then a voice yelled, 'ARRRRRRGH, MY PANCREAS!' It distracted Tornadia for JUST enough time for Ray to finally embrace her gift to bind.

As her own rainbow weather magic flooded through her body, Ray's hair began to glow. Every type of weather swirled and danced in the air above her before creating the BIGGEST rainbow anyone had *ever* seen.

Ray began to rise from the ground, her staff lifted high; the bright colours of the rainbow arched over her.

'HOW CAN YOU DO THIS?!' Tornadia screamed. 'How can you do this to one of *your own*?! *Another Rainbow Weatherling?!* You will NOT take my magic away!'

But Ray smiled sweetly and raised an eyebrow.

'I can. I will . . . and I HAVE!' she cried as she sent the large rainbow blasting through the air and straight through Tornadia's body. The Rogue gasped as Ray felt herself grip on to Tornadia's

power, deep within her very core.

'You might not want to be Rainbow Twist any more, Tornadia . . .' Ray shouted as she felt the Rogue's dark power rushing her way. 'But I will *always* be RAINBOW GREY.'

Ray kept on pulling at the dark magic as Tornadia stood frozen to the spot, helpless, illuminated by the green and blue glows of the Forever Crystals.

Ray felt the last drop of Tornadia's magic pour through the air and into her staff.

Tornadia fell to her knees.

Ray heard the voices of her ancestors sing inside her head as if they were right next to her.

For every bind,
You can not rewind,
But a little more peace,
The world now finds.

The scene around her began to warp and change and Ray found that she was also singing.

237

I will protect all around,
Some peace the world has found.
I will finish what I started,
In the Cavern of the Bound.

Ray blinked. She found herself in the dark cavern surrounded by the globes of bound magic. Then she felt something in her hand. It was a small, perfectly smooth globe the size of her palm. Swirling around inside the transparent ball were colourful wisps.

Rainbow weather magic. Tornadia Twist's magic.

Ray walked over to the lowest rocky shelf with Tornadia Twist's name plaque upon it and placed the globe of bound magic behind it.

'It's finally over,' she said to herself quietly. The scene faded and Ray was back in the Weatherstone Circle, her staff pulsing gently with green and blue light from the Forever Crystals. Tornadia was still on her knees, head bowed.

It was quiet and it was still dark.

Forecaster Flurryweather swept to the ground on the back of her cloud-unicorn, an army of Weather Warriors following close behind. They made their way towards Tornadia, binding her hands behind her back with one huge ice block.

Forecaster Flurryweather stood before Tornadia, looking down at the now powerless Rogue.

'Tornadia Twist, you WILL be punished,' she growled. 'You destroyed EVERYTHING. And I do NOT appreciate being trapped in a whirlpool of SNOT!'

Ray had never seen the head Forecaster so angry before. She'd always come across as calm and composed – vital for someone who plans all the weather on Earth.

'You will never be welcome in the Weatherlands again,' the Forecaster said darkly. 'And Precipatory Prison would be too good for you, even if you hadn't destroyed it.'

Ray tapped Forecaster Flurryweather on the arm gently. 'Um, Forecaster Flurryweather . . .

I was thinking . . .' she said quietly.

'What is it?' said the Forecaster, her cheeks flushed with anger. Ray saw a flicker of panic on Tornadia's face.

'Perhaps it's time Tornadia has a taste of what it's like to live with the effects of our weather magic,' said Ray. 'And Earth has prisons too.'

The crowd began murmuring among themselves.

Forecaster Flurryweather thought for a moment. 'If Tornadia is to live as a human prisoner,' she said thoughtfully, 'then maybe she'll eventually look up to the skies and appreciate what the Weatherlings do for Earth.'

'Aren't you forgetting something?' said Tornadia, as a sinister smile spread across her face. 'The pathetic Earth can't survive without the glowing Sunflower in the sky.'

'The Sunflower Fields and the school for SunKeepers are destroyed,' added another ember of the council. Forecaster Flurryweather looked to the SunKeepers.

'How about your Seeds of Hope?' she asked.

But the Sunkeeper who had lent her power to Ray shook her head sadly.

'What's a Seed of Hope?' asked Ray.

'Every SunKeeper in training receives a special sunflower seed,' the SunKeeper replied. 'It's their very own sun, which they hope to grow one day.

We kept them in a sparkly pouch hung next to our beds to remind us that one day we might provide the world with light.' She sighed. 'But when the School for Sunkeepers was destroyed, so was everything inside. Including our Seeds of Hope.'

'How about all your sunflower accessories?' asked Coo La La. He gestured towards the various sunflower headbands, wristbands or rings. 'How about one of those amazing sunflower wheels?! Can't any of those be used to replace the sun?'

'The big Sunflower in the sky must be grown from a seed and never picked,' said the Sunkeeper.

'So that's it?' said Droplett quietly. 'No sun ever again?'

The SunKeepers bowed their heads and took each other's hands.

Ray swallowed hard. This couldn't be it. She turned to Tornadia who was grinning widely.

'If you'd *just* handed over your magic, none of this would have happened, Rainbow Grey,' she said with a smirk. Ray blinked back tears. 'I may not have won,' said Tornadia, her eyes dark, 'but I didn't lose either . . .'

'No,' breathed Ray.

'What would your silly little friend La Blaze think of all this, hmmm?!' said Tornadia, relishing Ray's pain. 'I imagine she'd be incredibly disappointed in your EPIC FAILURE.'

Ray felt anger bubble furiously in her belly. In her toes. In her fingertips. In an attempt to control the fury rising in her chest she looked up and saw La Blaze's star glittering in the dark sky.

I really did try my best, she thought, closing her eyes and seeing La Blaze's face in her mind.

Her voice echoed in Ray's memory. *I've always wanted to be the STAR of the show . . .'*

Ray's eyes pinged open. She looked up at the dark skies sprinkled with twinkling specks . . .

Ray ran towards the Rainbow Weatherstone in the centre of the circle – the only stone still standing – and shouted 'BEARD!' at the top of her voice.

'Ray?! What are you doing?!' cried Snowden.

244

The large, swirling rainbow doorway appeared, and she leaped through it.

'RAY?!' called Droplett, 'Where are you going?'

Inside the burrow, Ray ran to the piles of paper tangled among the tree roots and picked up a small box with a painting of a sunflower on it. Her special La Blaze memory box. She opened it and saw the small, sparkly pouch.

Ray opened it carefully.

And there it was. Nestled in a pile of sparkling sunflower soil sat La Blaze's Seed of Hope. Their *only* hope.

CHAPTER 24

SEED OF HOPE

'We *will* light up the Earth and skies again!' cried Ray running out of the Rainburrow and holding up the shimmering seed. The SunKeepers gasped.

'It's La Blaze's Seed of Hope,' said Ray. 'Even though she didn't complete SunKeeper school, she'd kept it for all those years.'

'Can a new sunflower be grown with it?' asked Snowden hopefully.

'Growing a new sunflower from a seed takes years,' said the tallest of the SunKeepers. 'It takes a LOT of power. A lot of sun magic.'

'We can't leave the Earth in darkness,' said Forecaster Flurryweather. 'It cannot survive for much longer without light.'

Ray stepped forward. 'How about if all the SunKeepers use their magic together?' she suggested. 'Then perhaps I could channel ALL the sun magic using the Forever Crystals . . .

247

maybe, just maybe, that will provide enough power to help the sunflower seed to sprout quicker?'

'Ray, that's a lot of sun magic for you to handle in one go,' said the tallest SunKeeper, full of concern.

'Please, just let me try,' said Ray, holding on to the seed tightly. 'I HAVE to try . . .'

The SunKeepers looked to each other and nodded once before forming a large circle around the Rainbow Weatherstone.

Ray stood at the very centre, emptying the little pouch of sparkly soil at the base of the stone, and placing the seed into it carefully. She held her staff tight. 'I'm ready,' she said bravely.

As the SunKeepers activated their magic, Ray could see glowing lights everywhere – on headbands, rings, wheels, necklaces, glasses . . . The SunKeepers all used different sunflower objects to channel their magic safely, just as La Blaze always used her sunflower wristbands to channel hers.

Ray held out her staff. As the sun magic flowed from the SunKeepers into her, a warmth poured through her like the BEST feeling of happiness she had EVER experienced. Ray pointed her staff towards where she had planted the last Seed of Hope, letting the sun magic pour into it.

'COME ON!' Ray said to herself. She wasn't sure how much longer she could keep channelling the sun magic. It was so strong now, she felt as if she might explode. She could see that her skin was glowing brightly while the Forever Crystals in her staff were pulsating furiously.

As Ray worried about whether she could handle the magic, she felt a hand on her shoulder, then another and another. There were Snowden and Droplett, and her mum and dad. Frazzle and Fump. Nim.

Then something small and green popped out from the ground.

'It's working!' shrieked Droplett. 'You can do it, Ray!'

'You've got this, Ray!' cheered Snowden.

'May the light SHINE upon my feathers once again!' bellowed Coo La La, spreading his wings.

'Yesssss, Raaaaaaay!'

'Raaaaainboooow Greeeeeeeey!'

'YOU CAN DO IIIIIIT!'

The voices filled her head. She felt love all around her. Something even more powerful than magic. She focused ALL her energy on the tiny sunflower seedling, pointing her staff towards it, and with one almighty burst of colours, the stem erupted from the ground, stretching higher and higher, growing thicker and thicker, speeding up into the skies. The flower began to form at the top, petals unfurling around it. Finally, the big, glowing Sunflower in the sky bloomed and began to shine brightly.

The crowd erupted with cheers and tears of joy and relief. Nim wrapped himself around Ray, flying her up into the air above the happy crowd.

'RAINBOW GREY! RAINBOW GREY! RAINBOW GREY!' they sang together.

Below, Tornadia bowed her head in the new sunlight, and Ray wondered what she was thinking.

The five SunKeepers who had looked after the previous Sunflower took their places around the base of this new sun. They closed their eyes and reached out, allowing their magic to flow freely through the new glowing Sunflower in the sky. The Earth's brand-new sun.

We did it, thought Ray. The sun was shining brightly once again. Life on Earth and in the Weatherlands would continue!

Snowden and Droplett couldn't stop smiling. 'That was amazing!' cheered Droplett, fist-pumping the air and accidently sending a stream of water all over Snowden.

'Sorry!' she said sheepishly. 'I'm going to have to remember not to use my magic until I have a new rain cape!'

'We knew you'd do it, Ray,' said Snowden, still smiling while trying to dry off.

Frazzle and Fump did a little wiggle of joy, lightning glittering and thunder humming. 'Does this mean we're part of your gang now?' said Fump hopefully.

Ray chuckled. 'Everybody is part of it. I couldn't have done ANY of this without you guys. I needed your magic to make *my* magic! Thank you all.'

The friends hugged again.

'Y'know what sucks the most, though,' said Snowden. 'The Sky Academy is NO MORE.'

Droplett looked at Frazzle and Fump, then the three of them cheered. 'YAY! NO SCHOOOOOL!'

'Oh, I don't think so,' chipped in Forecaster Flurryweather. 'We will find a temporary base until we can rebuild the school.'

'At least we'll get LOADS of time off until it's finished!' giggled Droplett.

'Well,' Ray remembered, 'there *is* a whole other school right under where we're standing now. It used to be the Rainbow Academy, but maybe we could make it the new Sky Academy?'

Droplett groaned. 'Ray! We almost had NO SCHOOL!' She gave Ray a friendly nudge.

'Billowing breezes, I think that's an incredible idea!' said Forecaster Flurryweather.

Snowden's ears were positively bursting with snowflakes as he bounced up and down on the spot. 'Ray, you are the best!' he shrieked. 'The thought of no school for so long was making me itch.'

'We must have an Eclipse!' announced Forecaster Flurryweather. 'Every new Sunflower in the sky must be greeted with an Eclipse. A time when we all come together, and weather magic can thrive at its strongest, connecting us all.'

Ray felt the warmth of the new Sunflower in the sky on her skin. 'La Blaze's Seed of Hope,' she said quietly. 'I wish she could see how beautiful her sunflower is.'

'Oh, she can,' said Coo La La, perching on Ray's shoulder. 'You know, I can't actually believe it. La Blaze isn't even physically here, and somehow she stills comes out of this a hero . . .'

Ray chuckled.

'She's a star in more ways than one,' said Droplett.

'Yep,' said Ray. 'She really is the STAR of the show.'

CHAPTER 25

A NEW GENERATION

Six months had passed since Ray had bound
Tornadia Twist's magic. Everyone in the sky
had been working together to rebuild the
Weatherlands, and the new underground Sky
Academy was in full swing as a brand-new
term began.

Tornadia was safely on Earth, serving time for
her actions in a prison by the sea. Rumour had
it she was getting very good at sewing and Ray
hoped she was sorry for her despicable deeds that
had almost ended the whole world.

'I still can't believe we're SECOND YEARS!'
said Ray with an excitable giggle as she munched
on a lightning scone with a dollop of skyberry
jam on top. Ray, Snowden and Droplett sat in the
large lunch hall (which had been hidden behind
one of the many mysterious doors). Students sat

upon soft cloudy seats at arched rainbow tables. Ray waved at Slap and Streak, the thunder 'n' lightning bakers, who now worked in the school kitchen serving delicious weatherly dishes and the best rumblebuns!

A group of nervous-looking first years walked slowly into the hall, huddled together. One of them clutching a curly crook and hugging his cloud-ferret caught Ray's eye. She smiled and waved. Suddenly the child's eyes lit up. The group of first years waved back enthusiastically and suddenly they didn't look so nervous as they trundled up to the lunch counter.

Coo La La studied his reflection in the back of a spoon and sighed. 'I still can't believe I lost my hat. It made me feel so important. Now I just feel like . . . a pigeon.'

'But you ARE a pigeon,' said Snowden.

Coo La La turned to Snowden and narrowed his eyes. 'You know what, young Weatherling?' he said curiously, 'I'm rather baffled. I lost my best hat in all of that terrible weather, but I never

258

once lost my monocle. And never once did your glasses get swept away either . . .'

Snowden considered this and shrugged. 'You have a good point, and that is one conundrum I cannot answer.'

Coo La La moved swiftly on. 'So, I still think we need to combine our powers of genius. Why don't we start a club? OR put on a show! We could call it "AIN'T SNOW WAY THAT'S POSSIBLE . . ." where you invent new snow tricks and try them on me . . .'

The friends fell about laughing.

'I think RAY should start a club!' said Droplett. 'For rainbow weather magic, so we can ALL learn more about it!'

Ray let out a long whistle. 'There's still a lot *I* need to learn first,' she said with a grin.

Snowden tapped Ray's staff. 'But with those Forever Crystals you can finally use your original gift!' he said excitedly. 'Do you think you'll change your name to Rainbow Bind?'.

'Oh no,' said Ray. 'I'll always be Rainbow

259

Grey.' She pulled out her staff from the strap on the back of her rainbow waistcoat turning it around and around so that the Forever Crystals caught the light of the sunflower lanterns lining the walls.

'What I want to know is why a human boy called Klaus had the Sky Crystal in his rock collection?' pondered Coo La La.

Ray suddenly remembered something *very* odd from their trip to 78 Nettle Drive.

'His eyes!' she blurted out.

'Yes, he did have eyes . . . Don't most humans?' said Coo La La in surprise.

'They were like MINE!' she cried. 'One eye was purple and one was blue . . . like ME!' Ray sat up up a little straighter. 'AND he could understand YOU! Only *Weatherlings* can understand pigeons!'

'Guys. You don't think . . . Klaus can't be . . . a *Weatherling*, can he?' Droplett spluttered. 'Of course not, he has no magic,' Snowden added.

Ray's mind was spinning like a tornado. 'I'm

a Weatherling and there was a time I had no magic . . . My mum still doesn't have magic, just like everyone on that side of the family for the past one thousand years . . . remember?'

'Well, yes, but you were *living in the sky* . . . AND your dad is a Cloud Weatherling. Weather magic was IN your blood at least,' said Droplett.

'Think about it . . .' said Ray, getting up and pacing around the hall. 'A thousand years

ago, Rainbow Beard said that ALL the Rainbow Weatherlings who lost their magic to the Shadow Essence released by Tornadia *stayed on Earth* . . . Only Rainbow Beard returned to the Weatherlands. He's *my* great ancestor, that's why *I* was born in the sky. But maybe, just maybe, there are still generations of magic-less Rainbow Weatherlings on Earth?'

'But it's not really any good if they have no magic,' said Coo La La. 'You were all right because you found the big lump of Shadow Essence with rainbow weather magic trapped inside it.'

'I did . . .' said Ray. 'But I also have the magic of LOADS of Rainbow Weatherlings inside me and all of their gifts. Rainbow Weatherlings are only meant to be born with ONE unique gift.'

'Ray?' Snowden said cautiously, although he was smiling. 'What are you suggesting?'

'Perhaps I could *share* my rainbow weather magic with another true Rainbow Weatherling. If Klaus really IS descended from the ancient rainbow clans, then surely during the new Eclipse in a few

262

days would be the perfect time to unlock
his power?!'

A day later Ray, Droplett and Snowden stood at
the door of Number 78 Nettle Drive, England.

Klaus opened the door and squealed with
excitement. 'You came back!' he cheered. '*And*
you switched the sun on again!' He pointed to
the sky. 'Does that mean you beat the evil storm
lady?'

'Indeed we did!' said Ray with a grin. 'But
there's another reason we came to visit you . . .
Um, how do I put this . . .?'

'We think you might be a Rainbow
Weatherling . . .' said Coo La La simply.

The boy looked at Ray, Snowden and Droplett
blankly then burst out laughing. 'ME?' he
spluttered. 'I'm not a Weatherling . . . I'm Klaus
Bottomly.'

'Well, do you fancy coming to the
Weatherlands to find out?' said Ray.

263

Forecaster Flurryweather swept down into the front garden on the back of her cloud-creature.

'WOW!' cried Klaus. 'IS THAT A CLOUD-UNICORN?!'

The head Forecaster dismounted and stepped forward.

'Well, he could see me before I landed, which an average human can't do . . .' she muttered, 'and he DOES have the odd-coloured eyes . . . This is a good start.' She cleared her throat. 'Mr Bottomly, could I please speak to your guardian?

Klaus shrugged. 'Er, sure.' He looked back. 'DAAAAAAAAAAAD!' he yelled.

A tall man who looked exactly like Klaus might look in forty years stood at the door.

'Oh, hello!' he said with a jolly wave. 'I'm Bert.'

'Ah!' said Forecaster Flurryweather with a knowing smile. 'My name is Forecaster Flurryweather and I am the head of the Council of Forecasters from the City of Celestia. Would you mind if we had a little chat about the weather . . .?'

CHAPTER 26

A VERY SPECIAL ECLIPSE

Another week had passed, and the whole of the Weatherlands were gathered around the newly rebuilt Weatherstone Circle to watch the very special Eclipse taking place at midnight.

'A brand-new eclipse!' said Snowden, unwrapping a drizzle-pickle sandwich. 'I didn't think we'd get to see an Eclipse for another eleven years. This is SO exciting!'

Droplett materialised from a huge puddle with the biggest SPLOSH ever, completely covering Snowden from head to toe in rainwater.

'As long as I'm friends with you, Droplett, I'm never destined to eat a dry sandwich,' he sighed. Then smiled. 'But I guess that's OK.'

'Look at my shiny new cape from my shiny new dad!' Droplett said with a grin, while spinning on the spot and knocking the sandwich out of Snowden's grip. 'It's an OLYMPIAN-level cape, so I can puddle-port even faster now!'

'And don't I know it,' said Gusty Gavin, holding his tummy and looking a bit sick.

'You'd better get used to it . . . *Dad*,' said Droplett, giving the Wind Weatherling a friendly punch in the arm. She looked at Ray and Snowden. 'Having parents is WAY more fun than I thought it would be!' she said with a cheeky grin.

Ray couldn't have been happier for Droplett. And the underground Rainbow Academy had now become the Weatherling Academy (after many heated discussions with a certain pigeon as to why it could NOT be named the Coo La La'cademy).

Ray had decided to carry on wearing the Rainbow Weatherling waistcoat from long ago, complete with a brand-new embroidered emblem on its front pocket, courtesy of Snowden's excellent sewing skills. The Weatherling

268

Academy emblem looked just like the Sky Academy symbol, but now there was a rainbow stretched over the top. Where it should have been all along.

Ray stood inside the Weatherstone Circle, holding hands with Klaus. The boy hadn't stopped grinning since he'd arrived in the Weatherlands. Forecaster Flurryweather had explained EVERYTHING, from the existence of Weatherlings to the types of weather magic and how the Bottomly family were *definitely* descendants of the lost Rainbow Weatherlings from a thousand years ago. Klaus's dad had drunk fifteen cups of tea and dunked at least twenty-five custard cream biscuits by the end of the conversation.

'I'm so proud of you, son!' shouted Klaus's dad from the crowd. He and Haze had got on VERY well. While Haze explained how his cloud magic worked, Bert explained how a flip-flop is meant to be worn on your foot rather than your ear.

269

Ray's mum had been bouncing up and down on the spot for the past hour in an excitable frenzy. 'I LOVE YOU, RAY-RAAAAY!' she shouted above the chitter-chatter of the crowds.

Ray waved at Cloudia Grey, whose blue and purple eyes shone in the sunlight. Just like Ray's . . . Then Ray had quite possibly the BEST idea she'd ever had . . .

She ran over to her mum and dragged her into the centre of the Weatherstone Circle. 'Ray? What are you doing?!'

squeaked Cloudia. 'It's almost time for you to share your magic with Klaus. I'll need to get out of the way when the Eclipse starts!'

'It's starting!' yelled Droplett from across the crowd.

But Ray held on to her mum's hand tightly. 'How do you fancy sharing some magic with me too?' she said with a big grin on her face. 'You were meant to be a Rainbow Weatherling after all!'

For the first time in Ray's life, Cloudia Grey was lost for words. Her eyes welled up and she hugged Ray tight.

The crowds watched as the Moon King danced into view across the light blue sky holding his plate of round cheese. Ray felt her mum clutch her hand tighter, and Klaus clutched her other hand. Nim mewed and wrapped himself around Ray's shoulders.

Slowly but surely the big, glowing Sunflower above them began to dim, as the Moon King commenced with the new Eclipse.

'Today marks the beginning of a new era,' sang the voice of Forecaster Flurryweather. 'We have eclipsed the new big Sunflower in the sky. Every eleven years on this day we will mark this Eclipse. And we will invite the Woodlings to join us too.'

It was almost completely dark now. Ray looked up at the sky and saw La Blaze's star twinkling with all the other Sun Weatherlings of the past. As the Moon Cheese completely covered the sun, Ray felt a familiar rush of magic. The same rush she'd felt the day she received her rainbow weather magic.

The night sky filled with wisps of bright greens and pinks.

'The Aurora!' said Ray happily. She knew then that La Blaze and Rainbow Beard were there looking down upon her – gazing upon the beginning of a new generation of Rainbow Weatherlings.

Colours rushed through Ray's mind, and her gifts flashed before her eyes. She felt a special connection between her, and her mum and Klaus. A bond like no other.

273

The three Rainbow Weatherlings began to levitate high above the ground. Colours were pouring from Ray's chest into her mum and into Klaus, their hair slowly changing colour. There was one final flash of multicoloured light, and the three Weatherlings touched down. The new Sunflower in the sky was glowing brightly, and the air was calm and sparkly.

'Did it work?' asked Klaus, flexing his hands.

Ray looked at the boy with multicoloured hair,

then up at her mum, Cloudia Grey, whose large mop of hair now shone all the colours of the rainbow, just like her daughter's.

'Does it suit me?' asked Cloudia with a cheeky grin.

'It's almost as if you were MEANT to be a Rainbow Weatherling ALL along,' Ray winked, before hugging Cloudia and Klaus tightly. 'I'M SO HAPPY IT WORKED!' she cried.

Never in a windillion years had Ray imagined she'd one day be standing with others just like her.

'Oh, man, I can't WAIT to find out what my gift is!' squeaked Klaus, who then sneezed, causing a large rainbow cloud to erupt from his bottom.

The children fell about laughing.

'Well, that's a *very* interesting gift you have . . .' said Ray.

'That's SO awesome!' bellowed Klaus. 'I guess you can call me Rainbow Burst?!'

Ray and her friends spent the rest of the evening partying at the Weatherstone Circle and eating FAR too many rumblebuns. It was quite possibly the best day Ray had ever had.

As the new Eclipse celebrations started to round up, Ray sat with Snowden, Droplett, Klaus and Coo La La on Nim's floofy back, floating above the City of Celestia. The friends gazed down at all the repairs in progress as the people of the Weatherlands worked together to fix their extraordinary home in the sky.

'Thanks for sticking with me through . . . well, *everything*,' said Ray.

'You've got no choice. We'll ALWAYS stick together,' said Droplett.

'No matter what,' said Snowden.

'Unless one of you has the lurgy, then I'm going nowhere near you,' Coo La La added before tipping his brand-new, very flamboyant top hat.

Ray lifted up both hands.

'GROUP HIGH FIVE!' she cheered.

All of the friends completely missed. But Ray wouldn't have it any other way.

'Do you think there are others like me living on Earth?' asked Klaus as the new sun shone brightly down on them.

'Probably,' Ray replied, grinning at the thought.

'Can we go find them all?' said Klaus.

Ray chuckled. 'We can try,' she said. 'But for now, let's just enjoy today.'

THE END

ACKNOWLEDGEMENTS

Well, would you look at that. The third and final Rainbow Grey book is upon us and what a WHIRLWIND of a journey it has been. Having first come up with the concept for the magical rainbow-haired girl and her fluffy cloud-cat over ten years ago, I could never have imagined she'd have her very own series. I have so many wonderful humans to thank for making this happen. I know it's super gushy to say, but seriously, I wouldn't be where I am without you all. Yes, that includes YOU, the reader.

Firstly, a hurricane-worthy thank you to my agent Helen Boyle for, well, everything. Not to be biased, but Helen is simply the best agent anyone could hope for, and I'm not sure what I did in a past life to deserve her, but gosh, I must've been good! THANK YOU Helen for dealing with my mini mental breakdown throughout that weird year of 2020 . . . That was the year I started work on Rainbow Grey book 1. I can safely say, at one point, I was more than ready to hand the contract back to my publishers. I've never experienced such a creative block in my life. But Helen was always reassuring me that I COULD write this book even when I couldn't see the rainbows through the dark Rogue-ish clouds.

A super special thank you to my editor (and fellow Waterlow Park bagel-buddy!) Sarah Levison. I'm sure I must have given poor Sarah a few minor heart attacks throughout Rainbow Grey's first year, but she has been SO patient, kind and understanding. I have never known someone so wonderfully accommodating. And thank you to my publishing director Lindsey Heaven, an absolute marvel and fellow Essexonian. I'm so grateful for everything you've done, and delighted that you wanted to publish more books with me. I am also eternally grateful to Ali Dougal, who believed in from the very beginning of my Amelia Fang days. Without your faith in me, Rainbow Grey wouldn't even exist.

Over 2020, Helen, Sarah and Lins would set up Zoom calls to ease my nerves and help through any doubts I had during my first year writing Rainbow. You have always been there to shine light on a rainy day. Almost three years on, I am so proud Rainbow Grey now has a special home with you.

Thank you to the terrific and absolute genius of an art director that is TORNADO TIFF! Tiff always works above and beyond, laying out all of my illustrations with me (while we munch on Florentines and apple-sized grapes). Tiff is one of the most enthusiastic and kindest people, with such a passion for art. And, I must add, BRILLIANT taste in shoes

A huge thank you to Mum and Dad, and my younger but taller sister, Marie, who all listened to me moan about how rubbish I thought my work was on one day, then how much I loved author life the next. (Gosh, I must've been so annoying!) But they surrounded me with nothing but love and support. Mum would check in every day asking how Rainbow Grey was going and offering to listen to snippets, while Dad provided suitably dad-worthy weather puns when I needed them. And Marie has been a constant inspiration for our whole lives together.

Then there's Jamie Littler – my partner in crime, who had to live with me through my year of creative block. (And the poor man couldn't even escape because we were in lockdown!) But Jamie supported me ONE THOUSAND per cent, listened to me read the story aloud over and over. He was there every step of the way and I literally can't thank you enough, Mr Littler! (You also make the BEST cup of tea!)

A BIG blustery thank you to Lucy Courtenay for always doing such a wonderful job of proofreading all of my rambles, and to Melissa Hyder for working on this book. A special thanks to Cally Poplak for your lovely emails and continued support. Your messages of encouragement never fail to brighten my day!

The PR and Marketing team at Farshore really are most marvellous bunch. A HUGE thank you to Olivia Carson, Jas Bansal, Lexi Bickell, Liz Scott and Ben-Mallett-from-the-past. Every one of these fabulous humans has shouted about Rainbow Grey with such heart, and shared her story with the world. Thank you for always being so brilliant even when I'm mega slow to reply to emails (Sorry!).

THANK YOU to my fantastic publicists, from the past and present. Hannah Penny and Rory Codd who have both made tours, festivals and all things Rainbow Grey an absolute blast. I will never forget that epic stack of pancakes we had . . .

I also want to say a very special thank you to Siobhan McDermott, once my wonderful publicist, who saw Amelia Fang through from books 1–7, and the very beginning of Rainbow Grey. I'll miss our peanut-butter-popcorn-filled train journeys and Bake Off messages. Also, a big thank you to Hilary Bell, another past publicist who made travelling around on pumpkin-filled adventures such fun!

There will always be a special place in the city of Celestia for Gusty Gavin Hetherington – an almighty gust of thank yous for your constant support over my years of growing as an author and illustrator. And thank you to the glittering LJ Ireton, the ultimate book-display queen and one of the loveliest booksellers out there! A shout out to Katherine Stoyer and the super Rainer from the Ponds Beyond for your continuous kindness and always spreading your love for all things creative when it comes to Halloween and the weather!

And many rainbow wishes and much love to Grandad John, who I know would be so proud of my achievements.

THANK YOU to all my family, friends, booksellers, teachers, librarians, bloggers, reviewers and finally, to all the amazing readers. (Mostly for getting to the end of these acknowledgments . . .)

Even though this series started out a little bumpy, I channelled my inner Rainbow Grey . . . I didn't give up, and I got there in the end, because of all the wonderful people who stuck by me NO matter what. You all mean more than the earth and skies.

I shall round this up now! As Grandad John would say . . . Did, Done. Doings!

DISCOVER A WORLD OF MAGIC
BEHIND EVERY RAINBOW!

*Look out for something
NEW and exciting from
Laura Ellen Anderson –
coming next year!*

WEATHERLING
ACADEMY